An Unkindness of Ravens

A Shadow Thief Caper

By

David Lowrie

SHADOW THIEF: AN UNKINDNESS OF RAVENS
BY
DAVID LOWRIE

TEXT COPYRIGHT © 2022 BY DAVID LOWRIE
ART COPYRIGHT © 2022 BY DAVID LOWRIE

ALL RIGHTS RESERVED. THIS BOOK OR ANY PORTION THEREOF MAY NOT BE REPRODUCED OR USED IN ANY MANNER WHATSOEVER WITHOUT THE EXPRESS WRITTEN PERMISSION OF THE PUBLISHER EXCEPT FOR THE USE OF BRIEF QUOTATIONS IN A BOOK REVIEW.

10 9 8 7 6 5 4 3 2 1
FIRST PRINTING, 2022

ISBN 9798839967779

BLACK DOG GAMEBOOKS

BLACKDOGGAMEBOOKS@GMAIL.COM

Playing a gamebook

The chances are that if you have bought this book, then you will probably know what a gamebook is. If so, then please feel free to move on straight away to the next section.

If by some chance you haven't played a gamebook before, then it's basically interactive fiction. Most books are sequential. You start at page 1 and read page 2, 3 etc. until you get to the final page and the end and each time you read it, the book is the same and the story is the same.

In a gamebook, however, you make choices which indicate which way the story goes. The book is divided up into numbered sections. You start at section **1**. You read the text, and you are given the option of, for example, turning left, or turning right.

If you turn left you will be told to turn to a new section, let's say **142**. If you decide to turn right, then you are told to go to section **34**. Therefore, the choices you make determine which route you take through the book. I would say that you are the hero in your own story, but let's see, shall we?

As well as that, you also create a character, with different attributes. In this book there are things like fighting skill, endurance and agility. Your fighting skill helps you when you meet beings you may have to fight. Your endurance is how healthy or close to death you are, as you can easily die in this book - probably many times in many different but equally gruesome ways. If your endurance gets to zero, then unless told otherwise, you are dead and your adventure will end. This means you will have to start the book again – and maybe try a different route, or just be luckier.

Things like fights and tests are determined by rolling dice and adding them to different attributes. For this book you will need 2 6 sided dice (called d6). So if you are told to roll 2d6 – you roll two six sided dice and add the numbers together. If you are told to roll 1d6 – roll 1 6 sided die.

As well as dice, you will also need a pencil (not a pen!), a rubber and paper. To keep track of your attributes, which will change over time, there is an Adventure Sheet in this book which you can write on, or ideally photocopy so you can use them again and again.

I would also recommend using blank paper to draw a map, or a route through the book, as there may be times when the path is not clear and mapping where you have already been will help you immensely.

Of course, this being your gamebook now (as hopefully you have bought it from me) then you can ignore the dice rolling etc., and just read it and try to find your way through without worrying about dying. It's entirely up to you.

So, whichever way you choose, then I hope you enjoy your time playing this book. Any feedback would be much appreciated. If you get stuck, drop me a line and I will give you a hand (if you deserve it!).

BLACK DOG GAMEBOOKS

Or via:
Twitter: **Black_dog_gamesbooks @ BGamebooks**
Instagram: **blackdoggamebooks**
Email: **blackdoggamebooks@gmail.com**

The Facebook page will also keep you informed of upcoming gamebooks that I am in the process of writing.

Your character's statistics

Throughout your adventure you have a series of stats that will determine how good you are at fighting, how fortunate you are, how long you can keep going for and how quick you are. Each of these need to be generated by rolling dice and recording them on the Adventure Sheet in the book. These attributes will change over time – normally for the worst!

Fighting Skill

Roll 1d6 and add 6. This is mainly used in combat. It is how proficient you are with arms and in hand to hand combat. There may be weapons or other items that will enhance (or decrease) your **FIGHTING SKILL (FS)**. Your **FIGHTING SKILL,** can go above its original value with some additions.

Agility

Roll 1d6 and add 6. **AGILITY** is useful in lots of ways. In combat it helps you defend against attacks. In pursuits, or other times, then it can help you escape from enemies. It can also help you dodge traps due to your speed of movement. It can never exceed its original value, unless you are told otherwise.

Endurance

This is the ability of your human form to carry on and take wounds. To find out your endurance, roll 2d6 and add 12. If your **ENDURANCE** gets to 0 during a game, your physical form is dead, and your adventure is (most likely) over. You will have to start the book again.

Fitness

To find out your **FITNESS**, roll 1d6 and add 6 to the score. Fitness is your ability to keep on running, moving or fighting despite your all too human body getting tired. If you are in a fight, the longer it goes on, then the more fitness has to do with it – as you get tired and so are less able to attack and defend effectively. Fitness will go down by a point after each round of a fight or pursuit. However, this is only temporary, and it will return back to full levels by one point each subsequent paragraph. So if you go into a second fight soon after a first, you will be less able to fight.

Intelligence

This is the ability to think and reason. The higher your **INTELLIGENCE**, the more likely that you may be able to escape traps, outwit enemies and work out the logical puzzles. Roll 1d6 and add 6.

Fortune

This is the most random of characteristics. Sometimes pure chance will decide your fate. Some items you find may help (or hinder) your fortune so be careful when deciding what you want to take with you. Each time you test your fortune, subtract one from your **FORTUNE** score if you fail – as luck is fickle, and good fortune does not last. To find out your initial fortune, roll 1d6 and add 6.

An Unkindness of Ravens

Adventure Sheet

Fighting Skill	1d6 + 6	
Agility	1d6 + 6	
Fitness	1d6 + 6	
Intelligence	1d6 + 6	
Fortune	1d6 + 6	If you fail a FORTUNE roll, reduce your fortune by 1
Endurance	2d6 + 12	

Skills (pick 5)	Items	Notes

Combat

OPPONENT	FS	END
Name		

Shadow

END	FS

OPPONENT	FS	END
Name		

Shadow

END	FS

OPPONENT	FS	END
Name		

Shadow

END	FS

OPPONENT	FS	END
Name		

Shadow

END	FS

OPPONENT	FS	END
Name		

Shadow

END	FS

OPPONENT	FS	END
Name		

Shadow

END	FS

Combat

OPPONENT	FS	END
Name		

Shadow

END	FS

OPPONENT	FS	END
Name		

Shadow

END	FS

OPPONENT	FS	END
Name		

Shadow

END	FS

OPPONENT	FS	END
Name		

Shadow

END	FS

OPPONENT	FS	END
Name		

Shadow

END	FS

OPPONENT	FS	END
Name		

Shadow

END	FS

Making Test your rolls

There will be (possibly) many times when you are told to test an attribute. Unless told otherwise, the normal thing to do is roll 2d6 and compare this to the attribute you are testing.

If you roll less than or equal to your current score in that attribute, you pass. If you roll higher, you fail and have to face the consequences. The act of rolling 2d6 may be the difference between life and death!

For example, if you **TEST YOUR FORTUNE**, roll 2d6 and compare that to your current **FORTUNE** score. If it is less than or equal to your current score, then you pass.

Combat

Combat is often avoidable, but sometimes inevitable. To get through this ordeal, there will be times when strength of arms or an iron fist are the only way you can proceed.

This type of combat is aimed at those who either haven't played many game books, or just want to have a quick play through. This is the same as a lot of game books, in that you and your enemy both have a **FIGHTING SKILL (FS)**.

You roll 2d6 for your character and add the result to your **FIGHTING SKILL**. Now roll 2d6 and add the resulting number to your opponents **FIGHTING SKILL**.

The one with the higher total has hurt the other and loses 2 **ENDURANCE** points. You continue until you or your opponent has 0 **ENDURANCE (END)** – and so is dead or defeated.

Skills

It's been three years since you were indoctrinated into the Guild of Thieves. In that time your rise through the ranks has been nothing short of remarkable. Still just out of your teens, you have a reputation as being one of the best thieves in the illustrious 800-year history of the Guild. You have pulled off some of the most infamous heists and theft in recent guild history and are one of the Guild Masters most trusted lieutenants.

Due to your promise and proven abilities, you have been given additional training in the Skills of the Masters.

During this time, you have mastered 5 of the Skills of the Master Thief.

You have done in 3 years what most do in 10 years. Please choose 5 of these skills and write them on your Adventure Sheet. They are divided into physical and mental skills. You can choose as all physical, all mental, or a combination of both

Some may help you in this adventure, some may not but will do in further adventures. So choose wisely.

Additional Skills

If you have previously played as Shadow and want to bring your character across to this book, you can chose 2 **ADDITIONAL SKILLS** to the 5 initially allowed.

The maximum number of **SKILLS** you can have is **NINE**.

Physical Skills

Speed and Agility: All thieves are agile and quick, but you have been given additional training to give you the agility of a trained gymnast. It also means that your body is subtle and limber, and you are able to often fall and land on your feet, or roll to reduce injury.

You are also able to move much faster than most people, both in reflexes and physical speed. This means you can often outrun opponents, or react quicker to allow you to get the first strike in.

Move silently and hide in shadows: Stealth is a vital part of a thief's skill set, and working predominantly after night you are at home in the shadows. You are able to easily slip into the shadows and seemingly disappear from view as if by magic.

Your training and clothing also allow you to move almost silently on most surfaces and to pass without leaving a trace – except in the most extreme conditions. Having lived mainly in the dark, you also have exceptional night vision. However, due to your overly sensitive vision, bright lights or environments can sometimes dazzle you.

Sleight of Hand: As a thief, you are able to distract people to steal, as well as palm items and seem to make them disappear. It's similar to street magic that you see performers in the market square fooling people with. You have spent your time running shill games to part fools from their money. To some, it appears like actual magic!

Lock picking: One of the first things you were taught was to pick a lock. You are able to open all but the most complicated locks in a matter of moments, and also know how to jam a lock to make it unopenable – even to someone with a key.

You are also trained in the use of corrosive potions that can help to dissolve the largest and sturdiest locks or barricades. Your trusty lock picks are sewn into the soles of your soft leather boots. Do not lose them, as your ability without them is limited.

Climbing: You are just at home on the roof tops as you are on the streets. Having lived on these rooftops for several hours a day most nights since you were a child, you have become an expert in climbing onto roof tops and scaling almost vertical walls.

Sown into the sleeves of your clothes are also "cat's claws" that you can quickly put over your hands to give you extra grip. However, given the majority of this experience was gained in the town, you are less at home climbing in the wild – although you will still have an advantage over most others.

Unarmed combat: Fighting is not the greatest attribute of a thief, who would rather use stealth, guile and distraction. You also have little love for blood, preferring not to kill, not for moral reasons so much as the attention it draws.

However, at times you may be cornered and fighting is your only option. You have been trained in various martial arts that give you an advantage whilst fighting most unarmed foes. However, there are limitations, and this skill will be of little use against an experienced and armed opponent. So try to avoid fighting. Unless it's the final resort.

Mental Skills

Charm and guile: As a thief, you may find yourself in a situation whereby the options are either to fight your way out, or talk your way out. Against armed guards fighting is unadvisable. However due to your promise, you have been given training in the manners and ways of courtiers, and educated to a much higher level than a common cut purse. This charm allows you to extricate yourself from many a perilous situation, and also the ability to con and persuade others to do what you want.

"Sixth Sense": Your additional training in paying close attention to your environment has given you the ability to sense or know when something is not as it seems. This can be useful for a number of reasons. You can often tell when a person is lying, or not who they appear to be. Similarly, you can often sense when a situation is just "wrong", such as a potential trap – physical or mystical. This sixth sense has alone saved your life on 7 occasions. However, this ability is limited when moving fast or using your agility as the environment moves too quickly for even your enhanced senses.

Chakra: You have almost complete control over your sympathetic and parasympathetic nervous system. You can slow your breathing and pulse to appear almost dead, you can enter a trance to reduce your need for oxygen, food and water, and you can use the natural energies of your own body to speed up the healing of minor wounds and sprains. However, when you are using this ability, it negates all your other skills – and so make sure that you only use it when it's safe to do so – or you have no choice!

Forbearance: This may not seem like a skill, but many a thief has ended up dancing at the end of a gibbet due to alacrity. There is a well-known saying in the Guild that "A hasty thief is often a dead thief". Regular mental training has given you the strength of mind to ignore potentially dangerous impulses, and you think nothing of waiting for hour upon hour for the right moment to strike. You have also trained yourself to keep your body subtle and responsive during times of inactivity, to avoid stiffness and cramping. You can also, despite being exhausted, often resist the temptation to sleep.

Divvy: As a thief you handle a lot of valuables – mostly stolen! However, you must always be aware that there are a lot of fakes around. A combination of experience, education and training has given you the ability to spot a fake.

Resilience: Being a thief is a dangerous line of work. You have to be mentally strong to force your body to cope with the stresses and strains of life as a master thief. This has made you stubborn and mentally strong, and resistant to influence and even physical risk.

Equipment

You start your nights work in your normal thief's outfit. You are wearing plain and unremarkable clothing in black and grey. All black looks suspicious whilst moving though the town. Your jerkin is of the softest and subtlest leather, and adds protection of a light suite of leather armour. A hood is hidden in the neck of the jerkin. Cat's claws are also sewn into the arms of the jerkin that can be used to aide climbing.

Your boots are also the softest leather, with added grip to the very soft soles to allow purchase when climbing whilst still allowing you to move with great stealth. Sewn into a false sole of your left boot is your set of lock picks. In the top of the right boot, there are a couple of small phials of corrosive potions.

You are armed only with a two long thin sharp stilettos, well-hidden in a scabbard along your back. They are perfectly balanced and can also be thrown. You also have a small length or wire with a hook, a 20m coil of lightweight slim rope, a collapsible bag for your loot, a handful of poisoned caltrops and 20 gold pieces.

You are carrying no provisions as you are not expecting a journey, but have some snacks to give you energy enough to give you a boost of 2 endurance points.

Tonight started just as practically every other night has done for the last three years – on the roof tops.

Eating food

If your endurance is getting low, you can get food to recover 2 **ENDURANCE** points. You cannot do this during a fight and you can only eat one meal per section.

Previous Character

If you have previously played as Shadow and want to bring your character across to this book, you can do so.

You can bring your characters attributes. However none of them can exceed 12 (except for **ENDURANCE** which cannot exceed 24). If you have bonuses from previous books giving you over this level, then that will not apply in this book.

As previously mentioned, you can also bring over your **SKILLS**, and also choose 2 **ADDITIONAL SKILLS**.

The maximum number of **SKILLS** you can have is **NINE**.

Are you now ready to start your adventure?

Then turn to Section 1

1

The suns are just dropping down over the horizon of the Scarlet Ocean and you know that in a few minutes it will be almost totally dark in the port area in the large, sprawling city of Laeveni. The city is the largest in the empire of the One True God, and contains the holy seat of power. Behind you, as dusk falls, the bells chime from the tall elegant spires of Amaldi City. Amaldi is the central Holy City that resides as an almost separate state inside its own walls in the centre of Laeveni, high on the hillsides. This separate inner city is surrounded by marble walls 50 feet high, and just as thick, and nigh on impregnable. And it is guarded by 5000 warrior monks and priest knights.

The bells chime to call the many priests, monks and acolytes to service in the many hundreds of churches inside the Amaldi walls. The light of the twin suns reflects from the tall marble walls, making the inner city almost seem to gleam. But you are miles away from such grandeur. You hope you will never see inside the walls of the Amaldi City again, as last time you barely escaped alive.

However, you ignore the bells and focus. This is still your favourite time of the day – when the whole night is in front of you. You carefully suppress the excitement you feel for tonight's job, as excitement leads to haste. You are again perched on top of the grain warehouse at the edge of the docks, watching your current prey. You have been watching for the last three nights, knowing that the merchant finishes work at sundown, and then meets fellow merchants in a wine shop for a couple of hours before returning home.

You see merchant Malombr as he leaves his office and warehouse opposite your vantage point on Dockside Way. Malombr's warehouse looks just like a ramshackle place on Harbour View near the main wharf. He takes time and care to secure his premises. Malombr is a precise man who is never careless. In his time in the town, he has never been robbed despite his wealth being well known. On one has even tried, apart from that one incident a year ago. However, he is also a man of routine – which means he is also predictable.

The wharf is getting increasingly lively and rowdy, with sailors in port drinking alongside soldiers, brigands, dwarves and many other creatures in the many dives along the docks. Greasy smoke from the numerous fireplaces and torches lighting the roads drifts up to your vantage point, and mixes with the other smells of a seaport: salt, rotting fish, rubbish, excrement and the stench of unwashed bodies. Some things never change, you think to yourself wryly, but also appreciating that the city remains unchanged. The docks on a winters evening are not for those with weak stomachs – and that's before you even try the swill most of the taverns pass off as beer.

He then makes his way away up Harbour View across onto the Street of Blues. He could easily afford to take a coach, but you know he enjoys walking through the filth ridden streets of the wharf. This is partly because he likes to see where he started off as a street urchin, and secondly as he is always on the lookout for a business opportunity and he finds walking gives him the best chance of noting them. He's not worried about run-ins with less desirables, as he's not alone.

As always he's accompanied by his two bodyguards, who are as always half a step behind him, flanking him. These man-mountains look at least half-orc. They are fearsomely muscled and heavily armed with serrated bastard swords sheathed at their hips, along with a number of smaller weapons. You know that a direct confrontation with them would lead to a quick, painful and messy death – for you. Brawn was not an option. As so often in the life of a thief, guile is required.

You follow Malombr and his guards on cat feet, running effortlessly across the rooftops and across streets. You are well-named as you pass like a shadow in the night. Then Malombr turned left onto Willow Street, and follows the road round into Pawnbrokers Avenue. He crosses the square to The One Eyed Rat wine house, leaving his bodyguards outside as the Rat is one of the few places that he doesn't need them. It's also a tavern used by the Thieves Guild.

You wait on the rooftops opposite on the junction with Main Street. You wait in the same position for two hours whilst the merchant eats, drinks and brags with his friends and rivals.

Even the refined area of the more residential areas still carries the stench of the port – although the wine in the Rat is infinitely better than that from the harbour side dives. Then Malombr leaves the Rat, walking quickly and with purpose back home. You get up to follow across the rooftops.

Turn to **73**

2

The events of the night have left you exhausted. You are normally a light sleeper, as most thieves are – always on the edge in case the Watch catches up with them.

However you have fallen into a deep sleep. No noise or disturbance rouses you, as you lie there, dead to the world.

Then rough hands seize you, and you are startled awake. However, the hands are strong, and there is a hessian rag forced over your mouth and nose. An acrid liquid is smeared on the cloth, and you are forced to inhale it.

Your senses spin. Your eyes blur. You hear voices but they are slurred. Your skin feels prickly. Your head swims. You drift into unconsciousness, and start to dream dark visions of chaos and despair.

Now turn to **187**

3

The hook flies upwards towards the tower, but it just falls short of the top of the battlements, and clatters against the stone wall. Falls down the wall slowly, and then gets snagged in a lower window. You try to free it by tugging on the rope but it's stuck fast. You curse to yourself and drop the rope. It falls off the roof and lands with half of it coiled at the foot of the tower.

Lose 2 **FORTUNE** points.
Also write down the Codeword **GRIFTER**

You now have no choice but to try another method of entry. If you haven't already, you can either:

Use the crossbow with a heavy barbed bolt, which has a sturdy wire attached to it. Turn to **71**

Try to get into the gardens behind the house and establish the pattern of the guards. Turn to **14**

4

If you lost more than 2 **ENDURANCE** points during the fight, write down the Codeword **FENCE** (unless you already have it).

The Dusk Devil falls to the floor. It cries out, not in anger, but more in sadness and fear, and then its crimson eyes flicker and close. Now you have chance to examine it, it looks different to other Dusk Devils. They are always all black, but this one has dark grey fur, with white whiskers. You look around the room and find there is a nest in the corner. It's made of sticks and branches, planks and twigs. You hear a mewling inside the nest.

If you decide to look inside, turn to **10**
If not, turn to **78**

5

A cry goes up, as one of the half-orcs spies you. Their orcine heritage gives them sharper night vision than most men. You turn and try and run, but they appear from all over and converge on you. Half-orcs may not be clever, but they are cunning and cruel when in pursuit of prey.

They corner you against a high stone wall at the back of the garden. You try to draw your sword to fight but it is soon knocked from your hand.

Their vicious saw edged swords rise and fall again and again, until their edges glisten dark in the moonlight.

TONIGHT WAS YOUR LAST ADVENTURE

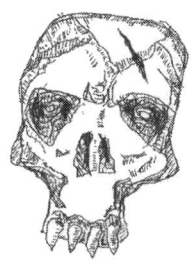

6

You nod in agreement.
"***Excellent***!" replies Lilith. She gestures someone forward.

If you have the Codeword **CON** only, turn to **128**
If you have the Codewords **CON** and **CARDSHARP**, if so, turn to **172**

Otherwise read on.

Two men walk forward. They are both regular looking men, of average height, with non-descript brown hair and unremarkable faces. One is in a black jerkin, and the other in a blue double-breasted jacket.

"These are Seth"(the man in black half bows, mockingly), ***"and Enoch"*** (the man in blue just stares down at you with icy eyes), ***"They will take you to where you hid this item. They are my most trusted lieutenants, and will have no compunction to slit your throat if you lie. Understand?"***

All reasonableness has fled out of Lilith's voice, which now sounds cold and emotionless.

Turn to **137**

7

You shout over at Brado "**How's your arm**"
He looks over at you and growls, but the whole of the tavern laughs. Lilith looks at Brado quickly, and away from the table. You take the chance to try to switch glasses.

She looks back and then pushes the glass on her left towards you. You decide to risk it.

If you have the **SKILL of SLEIGHT OF HAND**, turn to **21**
If you do not, turn to **191**

8

Your throw is true! The hook arcs through the night sky, high over the tower. Then it starts to fall, and it lands inside the wall atop the tower with a clunk. You pull on the rope and you can faintly hear it skitter over the stone roof, until it snags on a stone crenel. You tug it a few times until you are happy it's secure.

You calculate the angle of your swing in your head, and then jump.

TEST YOUR AGILITY. If you have the Codeword **CAT**, add 1 to your throw.
If you pass, turn to **98**
If you fail, turn to **177**

9

Desperately, you rummage around in your bag. Your vision is getting increasingly blurred, and your breathing has become laboured. You don't have much time.

You find the small hessian sack, and fumble at the strings, hoping that it will help you. Inside you find some fine grey sand that has an almost greasy feel to it, even though it passes through your fingers easily.

This is graveyard dirt, taken from the grave of a consecrated saint, shaman or sorcerer. When subject to certain complex (and dangerous) spells, it's turned into a cure for poisons. It works best when inhaled through the nose. There is only enough for one cure.

You sniff the dirt up, and then you are hit by a wave of pain so severe you nearly faint. Your body temperature rises to what feels like boiling point, your heart feels like it's about to explode, and your nervous system is on fire.

However the dirt burns the toxin out of your body.
If you lost any **FIGHTING SKILL** or **ENDURANCE** due to the toxins, you regain them now.
If you lose **ENDURANCE** due to injuries in battle when the toxin was in your blood, then you cannot regain these points.

Delete the Codeword **CUTPURSE** from your Adventure Sheet.

Return to the previous section that you were told to remember.

10

You peer inside, and see a small bundle of dark fur. You can see the small yellow eyes staring up at you in fear. Its small limbs are raised up, in a sign of submission.

It's an infant Dusk Devil! Now you know why the creature attacked you so violently. It must have been protecting its young. You guess given the different colouring that the grey Devil is the mother. You feel a surge of guilt, as you see the cute little animal mewling away. Lose 1 **FORTUNE** point.

If you want to take the Dusk Baby with you, turn to **70**
If you want to leave it, turn to **78**

11

Even with the sword, two opponents are too much for you. You fall to the floor, dead. Rough hands search you, and find the silk wrapped item.

TONIGHT WAS YOUR LAST ADVENTURE

12

Carefully, you search the room. The stories were true! The shelves are crammed with items used in dark magic. It had long been rumoured that Malombr had started to trade in such goods – which was a dangerous but highly lucrative business.

You examine the items, without picking them up.
Three catch your eye in particular. They are:

A left hand, severed at the wrist. In the palm, a short candle has been placed, with the fingers curved up to grasp the candle, to form a bizarre and disturbing candlestick. Wrapped around it is a piece of parchment.

Secondly, there is a small doll. It's made out of twigs and dressed in a patchwork of clothes. It has buttons for eyes, and its mouth is sewn up. It has hair made out of strands of what appear to be human hair.

Finally, there's a plain hessian bag. There a strange runes stitched on the outside, and it's no more than six inches square. In it is some grey dust.

You are thinking about which of them to take when you hear a scream from the room next door. It startles you into action, and you go to run out of the room. You only have time to grab one item.

If you took the hand, write down the Codeword **FINGER**.
If you took the doll, write down the Codeword **CHISLER**.
If you took the hessian bag, write down the Codeword **CUTPURSE**.

Then you hear another scream, this one of pure torment. It's definitely coming from the room next door. You run to the door. If you have the Codeword **CLIP**, turn to **51**
If not, turn to **87**

13

You decide it's time to leave the house, in case the Watch were alerted by the screaming. You leave the way you entered. However, you don't notice a dark figure hiding in the shadows outside, that sees you leave. The figure slips into the house and emerges a few moments later. Its eyes, the only part of its face visible due to the black hood and mask, narrow as it stares in the direction is saw you head towards.

It starts to follow, climbing to the roof, and keeping in the shadows, passing unseen, as it tracks your passage through the city.

Turn to **79**

14

It's not difficult getting into the garden, as it is a large expanse, and at the back are some tall trees and thick bushes. But as it gets closer to the town house, the trees thin out and are replace by a neatly cut lawn, with smaller, neatly trimmed shrubs. There are marble statues, and in the centre an ornate fountain.

You creep as close as you dare to the edge of the lawn and wait and watch.

You see no signs of the guards patrolling. You can now either:

Take a chance and dash for the back door, turn to **96**
Wait longer and try to discern the guard's patrols, turn to **27**

15

Despite the pain, you manage to pull yourself up, and grab hold of the sill with your other hand. You pull yourself up onto the ledge. Write down the Codeword **CAT**

Turn to **89**

16

If you have the Codeword **SOOT**, turn to **76** now
If not read on

You pick up the glass to your right, and Lilith picks up hers. She raises it towards you, and says "***Salute***". As its tradition, you clink your glasses together. Then she downs her whisky, and watches you.

Under pressure you drink your glass dry in one go.

"Anyway, I must be away. It was a pleasure talking to you.", she says, and stands and leaves. It was a strange encounter that leaves you somewhat perplexed. You cannot decide if you are sad that she's left, or relieved.

Write down the Codeword **FRAUD**

Turn to **91**

17

You wait a few minutes and then leave the tavern, choosing to exit via the kitchens and over the back wall into the back alley. You land lightly in the alley and then a dark shadow falls over you. You look around, and see a form still as death in the shadows. It moves out, all dressed in black, with only its eyes visible. The Raven draws his short sword as he steps out of the gloom.

You really shouldn't have used your true name, you muse to yourself, but then the fight is joined.

If you have the Codeword **FRAUD**, then you start to feel dizzy. You realise there was something in your drink. Lose 2 **FIGHTING SKILL** for this fight.

RAVEN	**FIGHTING SKILL**	**11**
	ENDURANCE	**10**

If you have the Codeword **FENCE**, after 2 rounds of fighting, turn to **61**
If you have the Codeword **CORSAIR,** after the first round of fighting, turn to **68**
Note down this reference.

If you win, turn to **66**

18

The orc drops to the floor with a thud. You sneak over, and carefully pull the dart from his neck. You smell it, and recognise the acrid odour as the poison from a Lepunia frog. It's lethal to humans, and only the half-orcs prestigious size had stopped him from falling dead within moments.

Then you hear a blood-curdling scream from the floor above.

If you want to go back up the stairs, turn to **24**
If you decide this caper is getting too dangerous and go to leave, turn to **186**

19

To be honest, she looks like she's handling the situation quite well as she's now got Brado's hand in a half nelson up his back. He grunts with pain, but you know he has a violent temperament and you don't want any trouble in Lecas' place, and so you walk over, saying,

"Brado, please leave the lady alone, she's here to see me"

Brado stops and starts to apologises profusely, between groans of pain. Not many people in the tavern know who you are, but they know that despite your slight build and youthful appearance, you have a reputation. And Brado doesn't want to get barred from the Rat.

Gain 1 **FORTUNE** point for being so gallant.

"I think you can give the man back his arm now, mi 'lady. Would you care to join me at a table? Would you like a drink?"

*"**Whisky, neat**"*, she says smiling. She lets go of Brados' hand and gives him a shove. He sprawls to the floor, and most of the tavern laugh. Brado gets up and sits back down, grumbling, and nursing his sprained arm. She walks over to a vacant table near the bar. She is slim and athletic, and she moves with a kind of lithe elegance, like a cat stalking its prey. You go and collect your pint, and order a whisky.

You return to the table and place the drink down. She sips it and nods her head in approval. **"An Inglea whisky! Good choice. The water flows through the peat bogs giving is a smoky taste. This taste to me like an Illacaol from the far north east coast of the island."**

You smile in agreement, incline your head, and raise your glass. In truth you have no idea, you just asked Lecas for a whisky. But then again, the old landlord was good at reading peoples tastes.

You take the chance to assess her. She's tall, taller than you, with raven black hair, cut to her shoulders in a bob around her face. Her fringe is straight and covers her forehead. She has a wide, pale face, high cheekbones, with warm brown eyes, a long straight nose, and thin lips – that always seen to be turned up in a sardonic half smile.

She is dressed in practical clothes, but of a fine cut. A black leather vest buttoned up over a fine silk shirt that billows over her arms. She is wearing black leather boots that reach mid-calf, and black satin trousers. At her waist is a thin silver handled rapier, and a thin silver dagger, hanging together beside each other.

She raises up her hand *"I must thank you sir, for extricating me from that situation. Although I was in no need, I was pleased I didn't have to break that man's arm, and your help arrived at the right time to prevent a less, erm, unpleasant an outcome. It's so hard to get a drink in a tavern when you have just killed on of the locals."* she smiles, fully this time. You cannot help but smile as well.

"I am Lilith", she continues, and then pauses, staring expectantly at you.

Are you going to tell her your true name, if so turn to **26**
If you want to say your name is Vostede Mesmo, turn to **42**
If you want to say your name is Jacs, turn to **55**

20

You decide that you cannot leave the merchant to be tortured by the Raven. You must intervene.

If you have the Codeword **FINGER**, turn to **54**
If not, read on,

You grimly draw your sword and creep into the room. You do not fancy your chances against a Raven, as they are experts with any number of weapons, but you hope you can kill him with a swift blow from behind.

TEST YOUR FORTUNE.
If you are lucky, turn to **157**
If not, turn to **171**

21

She didn't seem to notice the switch. You pick up the glass to your right, and Lilith picks up hers. She raises it towards you, and says *"Salute"*. As is tradition, you clink your glasses together. Then she downs her whisky, and watches you.

Under pressure you drink your glass dry in one go.

"Anyway, I must be away. It was a pleasure talking to you.", she says, and stands and leaves. It was a strange encounter that leaves you somewhat perplexed. You cannot decide if you are sad that she's left, or relieved.

Turn to **91**

22

You get half-way across and there's a sudden gust of wind. You struggle to keep your balance

TEST YOUR AGILITY AND YOUR FORTUNE, by rolling 4d6. If you have the **SKILL OF SPEED AND AGILITY** you can reduce the roll by **2**

If you pass, turn to **63**
If you fail, turn to **175**

23

You fall. Unable to find your balance you topple off the window sill and plummet to the ground beneath. Fortunately, you land in a thick bush, but it still hurts, and drives the breath from you. Lose 4 **ENDURANCE**.

TEST YOUR FORTUNE
If you are lucky, turn to **94**
If you are not, turn to **5**

24

The stairs go up to the first floor, and you can see two rooms. The door on the left is black, and the one on the right is white. Both are closed.

To try the black door, turn to **59**
To try the white door, turn to **88**

25

You decide not to intervene and to get out of this house as soon as you can. You go to exit, but as you do, the Raven sees you. His hand flashes to his weapons belt and he grabs three darts and hurls them. They thud into your back, and you drop to the ground as the quick acting nerve toxin has its effect.

TONIGHT WAS YOUR LAST ADVENTURE

26

"A most unusual name, but then again, this is an unusual world", she replies when you tell her your name is Shadow. Again she half smiles. *"I had heard of a small bird called Shadow who worked in these parts. Have you heard that?"*

You stay quiet, unsure if she knows you are the Guild Master of the Jackdaws. She doesn't seem to mind.

She stands up, saying,

"My round, I think."

Before you can say anything she heads to the bar. When she returns, she has two equally full crystal glasses of whisky. She places them next to each other on the table. Both look identical.

"After you", she says, inclining her head.

But first, write down the Codeword **DIPPER**.

If you are going to take the glass on your left, then turn to **31**
Or the glass on your right, turn to **16**
Or create a diversion, turn to **7**

27

It takes you some time, but you think you have figured out the pattern. There are 3 guards on patrol. The first one guard, who you have named Guard Angra, starts at the NW corner of the house. Guard Bagra starts at the NE corner of the house. Guard Cunga starts on the southern wall. You are looking at the southern wall from the garden and the door is in the centre of the wall, where Guard Cunga starts his patrol.

The house is 30 yards wide, from East to West, and 20 yards deep, from North to South. Each of the guards walks at exactly 10 yards per minute, as they are very particular about their patrol. In total, it takes the patrol 10 minutes to do a full lap of the house.

If you can work out which of these minutes has no guards at all on the south wall and so will allow you to get to the door unseen. If you can, work out of the sum of that number when added to this current section number.

If it is not clear when you turn to that section that you have made it across the lawn in time, then return here, and turn to **96**

28

You fail to notice as you open the drawer that it is booby trapped. Too late you hear a loud "**SNIKT**" and at the same time you feel a pin-prick on your hand that's opening the drawer. You look down and see a small bead of blood in the centre of the back of your hand. It's just a scratch, you think.

However in a matter of seconds the toxin takes hold. Your body starts to convulse, and you open your mouth to scream in pain but instead your jaw closes involuntarily on your tongue and bites clean through it. A fountain of blood cascades out of your mouth and over the desk. Your legs buckle, and you drop to your knees and look in

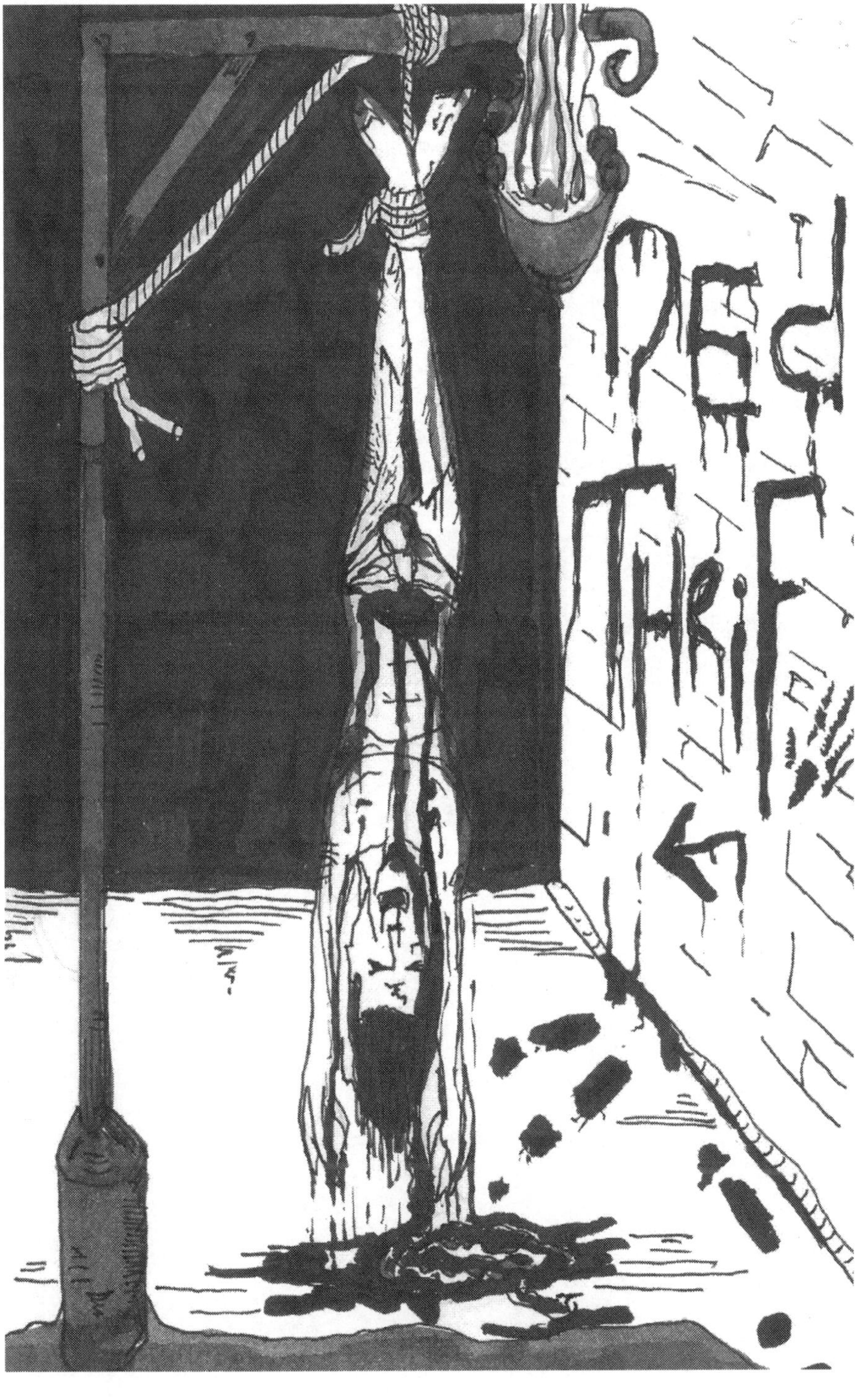

horror at your hand as it starts to turn a vivid purple. Then blood starts to pour out of your eyes, nose, ears and every other orifice.

You keel over and collapse on the floor convulsing until finally the toxin reaches your heart and causes it to explode. The noise of you thrashing around on the floor has alerted the house – and the last thing you see through blood red eyes is Malombr standing over you smiling.

Malombr calls his guards, and they come and drag away you inert body. They take your remains outside onto the main street and strip you to your loin cloth, and then place a rough noose of hemp rope around your feet and drag you do the nearest lamp stand. They fling the end of the rope over the crossbeam and pull. You are hoisted off the ground and left dangling above the ground with your blood still dripping down onto the floor.

One of the guards ties off the rope, whilst the other dips his fingers into a puddle of your blood, and writes on the wall in your own blood "**DED THEIF**". Your corpse remains strung up on the post for some weeks – and becomes a welcome meal for a lot of the scavengers that live in the city. Soon there is little left of you but yellowing bone, but you remain strung up there as a warning not to try to steal from Malombr.

TONIGHT WAS YOUR LAST ADVENTURE

29

If you have the Codeword **GRAFTER, TEST YOUR FORTUNE** now
If you lose, turn to **5** now
If you win, read on

You either worked out the pattern or were very lucky! Guard Cunga on the south wall takes a minute and a half to cover the 15 yards from the south door. Then he turns the south west corner and heads north, out of sight. You now have 30 seconds before Guard Angra, moves into view.

So now you have half a minute to get across the garden and in through the door.
You sprint across the lawn, and drop to your knees at the door.

TEST YOUR INTELLIGENCE. If you have the **SKILL OF LOCK PICKING** you can take 1 off the roll.
Each attempt to pick the lock takes 10 seconds. If you can do it in one or two attempts, turn to **80**
If it takes you three attempts, turn to **57**
If you still haven't picked it after three attempts, turn to **5**

30

You go to walk through the door. If you have the **SKILL OF SIXTH SENSE**, turn to **46**
If not, turn to **33**

31

You pick up the glass to your left, and Lilith picks up hers. She raises it towards you, and says "*Salute*". As its tradition, you clink your glasses together. Then she downs her whisky, and watches you.

Under pressure you drink your glass dry in one go.

"Anyway, I must be away. It was a pleasure talking to you.", she says, and stands and leaves. It was a strange encounter that leaves you somewhat perplexed. You cannot decide if you are sad that she's left, or relieved.

Turn to **91**

32

The bolt flies true, and thuds into the heavy oak crossbeam. Your keen eyes can see that it's buried deep into the wood, past the barb. You tug a couple of times on the wire, and the bolt seems to maintain its hold. You quickly secure your end of the wire around the sturdy chimney stack. You make sure it's taught, with only a little give.

You leap lightly up onto the wire and start to make your way across the perilously thin road. Your soft shoes wrap around the hard wire, and you try to use your toes to grip it. You start your difficult crossing. Then, all of a sudden a storm breaks out of nowhere. It's seasonal in Laeveni, but it makes your job a lot harder. The rain falls down, and forked lightning crashes from the sky. Hopefully the storm will be short lived.

TEST YOUR AGILITY. If you have the **SKILL of CLIMBING**, then you can subtract 1 from your roll.

If you pass, turn to **69**
If you fail, turn to **22**

33

As soon as you enter the room, you realise you have triggered something. Not a physical trap, but something magical. You look around, and see with horror that there is a wave of mystical force travelling up your body. It holds you still as it climbs up.

The energy flows up into your head, and you feel it start to expand. One eye throbs and grows to a huge size, whereas the other eye flies out of its socket with a pop. You start to bleed from your nose, and wax flows from your ears. Your tongue is almost ripped out of your throat and hangs outside your mouth, blistered and full of pustules.

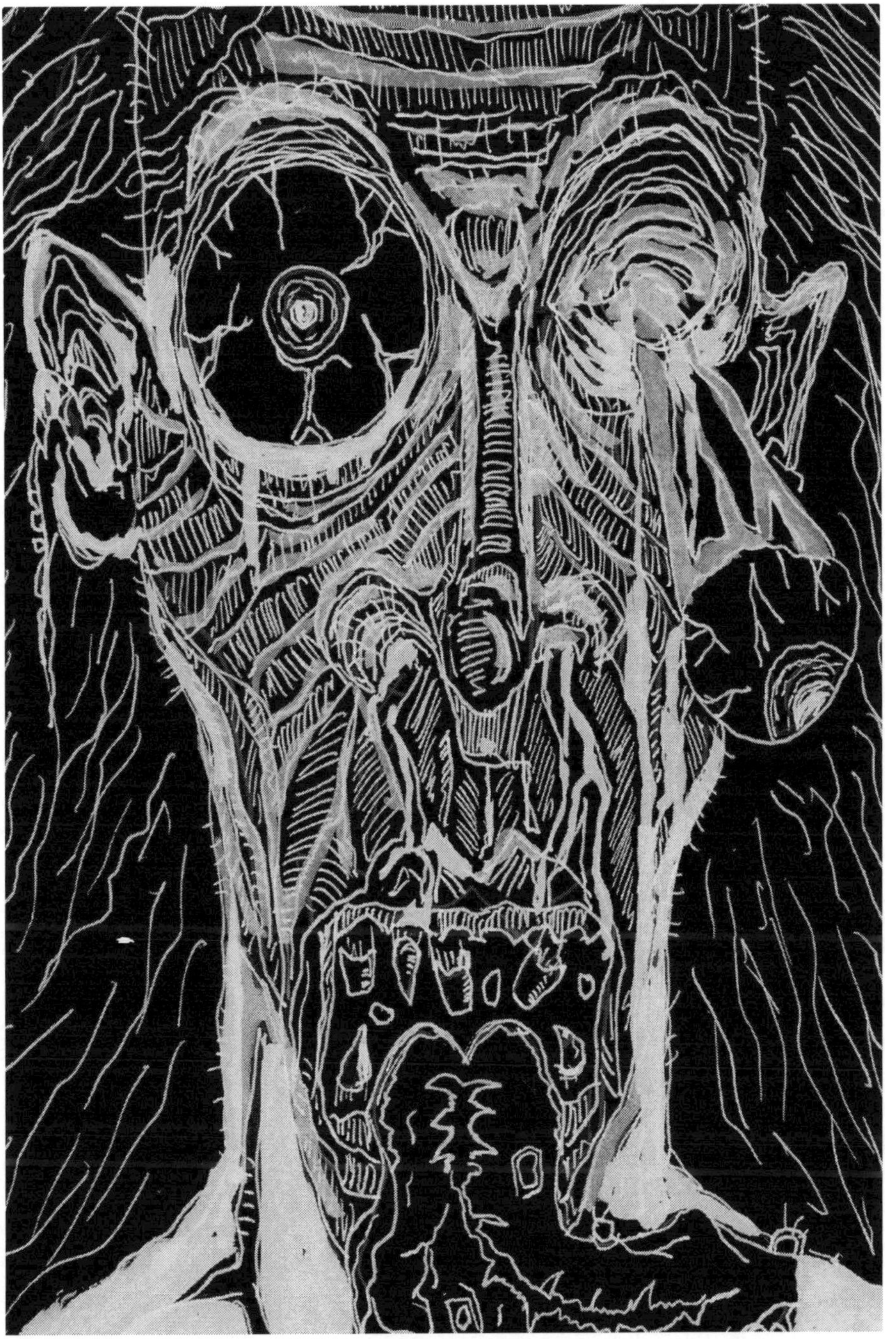

You skin starts to age, crack, and split. Your long, lustrous hair, falls from your scalp. The pressure in your skull increases, until the bone cannot contain it. Your head explodes, covering the room in bone, brains and blood.

Your headless body topples to the floor in a puddle of red, grey and white.

TONIGHT WAS YOUR LAST ADVENTURE

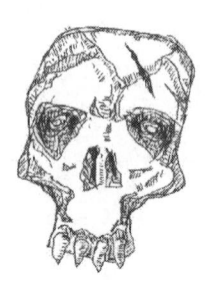

34

If you have the Codeword **GRAFTER**, turn to **5**
If not read on.

You slip quietly across the lawn and are about halfway across when you see a guard appear from the right hand corner. You stop dead still. The half-orc guards don't have much in the way of an imagination to distract them, and they don't easily tire, and so they are thorough in their task. This one beats bushes with a long halberd it is now carrying. Its pig like eyes scan the gardens for any sign of an intruder.

TEST YOUR AGILITY. If you have the **SKILL OF HIDING IN SHADOWS**, you can reduce the roll by 1.
If you pass, turn to **77**
If you fail, turn to **5**

35

Finally, you manage to kill the Raven. He falls to the floor, moaning. You wipe your blade on his clothes, and sheath it. Then you manage to cut down Malombr from his shackles and manhandle him to the bed.

He starts to moan in pain as he slowly regains consciousness. He murmur something, delirious in his pain. You go over and assess his wounds. Given time, he may recover, as most of the injuries are superficial, but painful. The Raven was careful not to administer any mortal wounds.

You grab the thick grease like ointment from the table, and spread it on his wounds that are still bleeding. He screams in pain, as the ointment stings the torn flesh, but it works. The blood starts to congeal. You also find a liquid for the pain, and give it to him. He starts to relax a bit but then passes out. You leave him sleeping.

If you have the Codeword **CAT**, you can also use some of the ointment on your shoulder, and this will alleviate your pain. You can increase your **FIGHTING SKILL** and **AGILITY** by 1 each.

You decide it's time to leave the house, in case the Watch were alerted by the screaming. You leave the way you entered

TEST YOUR INTELLIGENCE. If you have the **SKILL OF DIVVY**, you can remove 2 from the roll.

If you pass, turn to **39**
If you fail, turn to **13**

36

You have quite badly damaged your left shoulder, and must reduce your **FIGHTING SKILL** by 2, and your **AGILITY** by 2.

If you have the **SKILL OF CHAKRA**, then you can use this to reduce help heal your shoulder, and this will lead to you only having to lose 1 for **FIGHTING SKILL**, and nothing for **AGILITY**.

However, using Chakra is tiring and hard on your body. Roll 1d6. That is how much **ENDURANCE** you lose, as you are using your own vitality to heal yourself.

Now return to **41**, and read on.

37

Lecas gets pulled away from your talk to serve a large party of barbarians. There were only three of them, but they are still a large party. You stand at the bar, nursing your pint, taking the odd sip. The Goblin Basher is on form tonight. Light, with a good bitterness but a sweet malty aftertaste.

You stand there minding your own business, when you hear a voice behind you.

"Knucklehead, put that hand elsewhere before you lose it", says an angry female voice. You turn and see a woman who has been approached as she makes her way to the bar. She is incredibly striking: tall and athletic, with shoulder length dark hair. However, something makes you uneasy. It's as if she carries an aura of danger about her.

One of the locals, a sailor called Brado, has placed his hand somewhere inappropriate on her body.

Are you going to help her?
If you decide to, turn to **19**

If not, you decide to leave the tavern in case there's any trouble. You finish your drink and make for the back door, which leads to an alley at the side of the One Eyed Rat.

Turn to **192**

38

He can't regain his balance and starts to fall, but as he does, he manages to grab hold of your foot. You frantically try to grasp the ladder, but his weight is too much.

You both fall, and smash onto the hard cobbled stones below.

Enoch above hears the noise, and looks out of the attic. He sees you and Seth entangled on the floor, unmoving. Carefully he makes his way down the broken ladder, reaches inside your tunic. He finds the silk package, and walks off without a further look back.

Lilith will be pleased with him. He almost smiles.

TONIGHT WAS YOUR LAST ADVENTURE

39

You have sensed there is something in the room that's important. You quickly search the chamber, and see something odd about the bed frame. You hunt for a hidden catch, and find it and trigger it. A hidden compartment opens in the bed. Inside is something small and disc shaped, and wrapped in silk, and you place it in your bag. Well, you are a thief after all.

You decide it's time to leave the house, in case the Watch were alerted by the screaming. You leave the way you entered. However, you don't notice a dark figure hiding in the shadows outside, that sees you leave. The figure slips into the house and emerges a few moments later. Its eyes, the only part of its face visible due to the black hood and mask it wears, narrow as it stares in the direction is saw you head towards.

It starts to follow, climbing to the roof, and keeping in the shadows, passing unseen, as it tracks your passage through the city.

Write down the Codeword **FALCON**

Turn to **79**

40

If you have already been upstairs, you decide to leave the house by the front door. Turn to **79**

If not, read on,

You decide to head up the stairs. You take them carefully, and they curve around until they reach a landing half-way up. Straight in front of you is an half-orc guard. He is staggering around, with foam bubbling from his mouth. His eyes look confused, but then he sees you and snarls. He draws his serrated bastard sword, and lunges at you.

As he does, you notice a small black barb in the half-orcs neck. A poison dart!

However then he is on you and you must fight him. Luckily he's confused and weakened, otherwise this would have been a sterner test. Grimly you draw your sword, which looks like a short dagger compared to your opponents.

HALF-ORC BODY GUARD **FIGHTING SKILL** 7
                         ENDURANCE   8

If you have the Codeword **CORSAIR,** after the first round of fighting, turn to **68**
If you have the Codeword **FENCE**, after 2 rounds of fighting, turn to **61**
Note down this reference.
If you win, turn to **93**

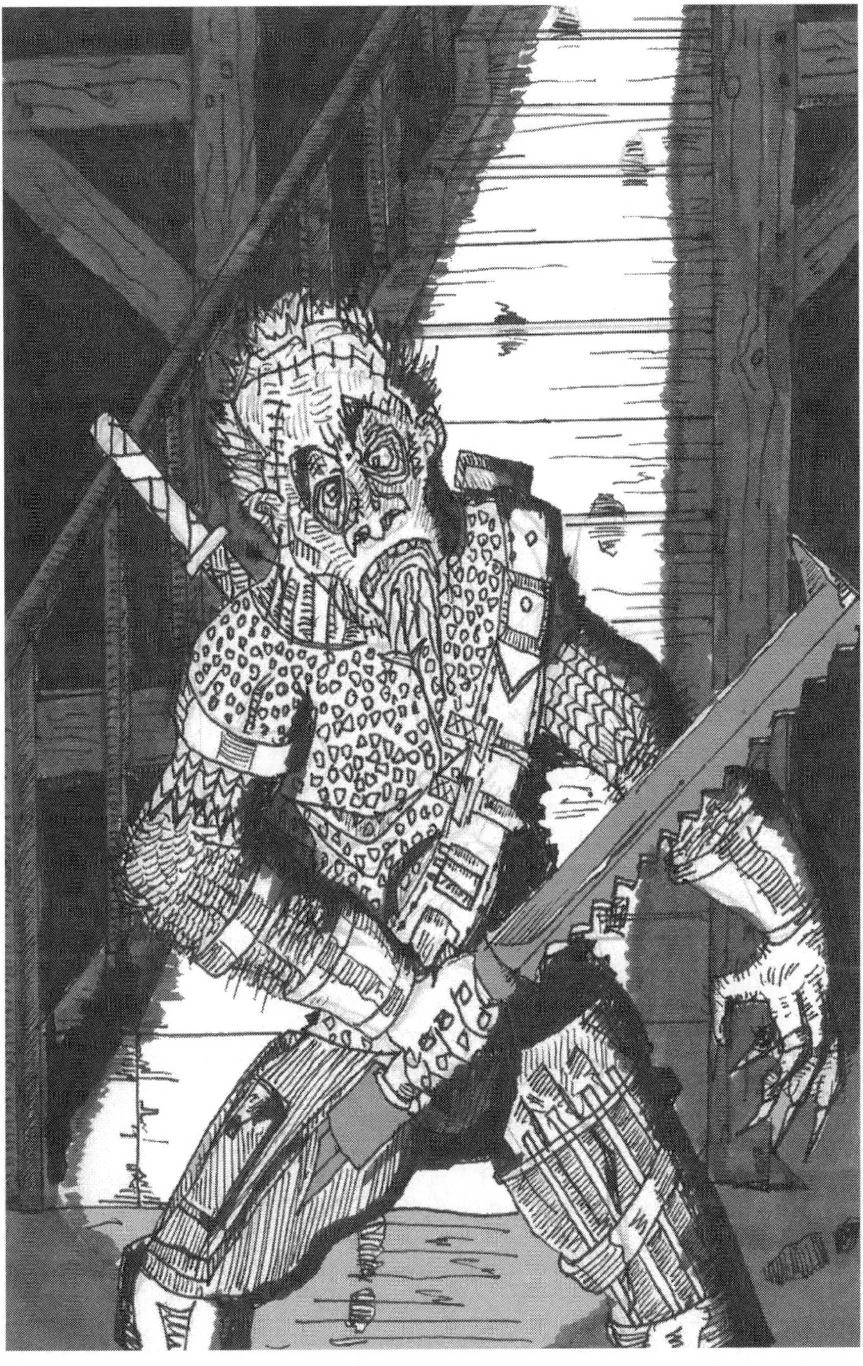

41

If you have the Codeword **CAT**, turn to **36**
If not, read on.

You are in a grubby room at the top of the house. It is all in dark, but your eyes quickly adjust. You can see shadowy shapes, covered with dust covers, and the floor is thick with dust.

TEST YOUR INTELLIGENCE. If you have the **SKILL OF SIXTH SENSE**, you can reduce the roll by 1

If you pass, turn to **83**
If you fail, turn to **53**

42

You tell her your name is Vostede Mesmo. You are pretty sure she won't have heard of the old veteran soldier and adventurer. She stares at you for a few moments, unsmiling and then she replies,

"Pleased to make your acquaintance. I recognize the name. I heard there was a famous adventurer and hero who had this name. Surely you are not he? This was some time ago."

"My uncle", you reply, possibly a bit hastily. *"I was named after him, although I do not favour him in looks or skill"*

"*Ah*", she says, half smiling.

She stands up, saying,

"My round, I think"

Before you can say anything she heads to the bar. When she returns, she has two equally full crystal glasses of whisky. She places them next to each other on the table. Both look identical.

"After you", she says, inclining her head. Then she pushes the one on her left towards you,
Turn to **16**

43

Some hours later; or days, mere moments, you know not; you stir. You don't open your eyes, but listen and feel and use all your other senses. The room is quiet but stinks of blood. Your body seems to be in surprisingly good condition.

Enoch was an expert. He knew how to administer the most pain with the least damage. But through pure mental strength and resolve, you had not been broken. They must have left you to recover, as a dead prisoner is an un-cooperative prisoner. You may not have much time.

You ache all over, and you are exhausted, but you flex your muscles as you sit and cannot feel any lasting damage.

Lose 4 **ENDURANCE** points due to the effects of the torture.

However, Seth has loosened most of the ropes, so that Enoch could work on the pain centres of your body. You run your long thin fingers over the knots tying your wrists, and feel that one has slackened. You manage to start to free your hand, but you cannot get the final loop over your right hand, and so with a grunt, you wrench your right thumb, dislocating it.

The pain is excruciating, but you manage to get the loop of rope over. Your hands are free.

If you have the **SKILL OF CHAKRA**, you manage to pop the thumb back into its socket. It hurts like hell, but there is no damage.

If not, then lose 2 **ENDURANCE** and 1 **SKILL**.

You manage to reach over to the table and grab a scalpel. You quickly cut away the rest of your bonds, and dress as best you can. Your other items are in the corner of the room. You grab them. There is only one door out, and so you sneak up to it and listen. All is silent.

You open it, and see a plain corridor. Along the left hand side is an open window. You run to it, and jump up and out.

If you have the **SKILL OF SIXTH SENSE**, turn to **101**
If not, turn to **179**

44

You use your smallest shiv to slip into the lock and it opens with a slight "**CLICK**" that sounds as loud as a banshee in the still night of the house. You stop and listen for a few minutes. Nothing.

You slowly pull the drawer open, taking care to look for traps or trip wires.

If you have the **SKILL OF SIXTH SENSE**, turn to **50**
Otherwise **TEST YOUR FORTUNE**
If you pass, turn to **195**
If you do not, turn to **28**

45

You pull back the curtains, and creep in. The room is lit by candles, and you wish it had been in darkness. The merchant Malombr is hanging from a chandelier in the centre of the room. He is naked apart from a loincloth. His hands are tied together and hooked over the chandelier. His feet are also tied with rope. His thin body is slick with blood and sweat.

In front of the merchant, facing you, is a figure clad in black. He is wearing tight fitting black hose, and a black tunic. His head is covered with a black hood and mask, so that you can only see his eyes. He has a short sword slung over his back, and a weapons belt at his waist.

The dark figures hand flashes to his belt, and his arm flicks. Three darts thud into your chest before you can move. The toxin is mercifully quick. As you die, the assassin turns back to the merchant, saying in a voice like silk,

"Now, good merchant, where were we?"

The screaming starts.

TONIGHT WAS YOUR LAST ADVENTURE

46

You are about to enter the room when you notice some runes on both sides of the door frame, about a foot up. You examine them closely without touching, and the air seems hot between the runes. Taking no chances, you jump over the hot barrier. The air behind you fizzles when you land.

Turn to **12**

47

Make sure you remember your previous reference, in case you survive.

The toxins in your body are now starting to take hold.
You now feel almost so weak you cannot stand, and you have a feverish temperature, and your whole body is shaking.

If you don't find a cure you will be dead in mere moments.

If you have the Codeword **CUTPURSE**, turn to **9**
If you have the **SKILL of CHAKRA**, turn to **194**

If you have neither, then your body succumbs to the toxin.

TONIGHT WAS YOUR LAST ADVENTURE

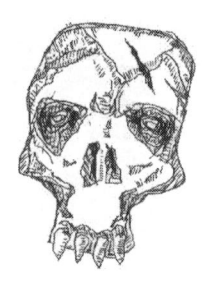

48

You uncoil the grappling hook from the long grey rope. You look around and see the tall tower that is across the street. If you can lodge the hook into the parapet of the tower, then you should be able to swing across to the townhouse.

Then, all of a sudden a storm breaks out of nowhere. It's seasonal in Laeveni, but it makes your job a lot harder. The rain falls down, and forked lightning crashes from the sky. Hopefully the storm will be short lived.

You stand right on the edge of the roof, and hold the hook loosely in your hand. You let it trail down a bit until you have a length of rope, and start swinging it round in a circle, underarm. You slowly let the rope feed through your hands, so the circle increases.

Then when you are ready, you let fly.

TEST YOUR FIGHTING SKILL and FORTUNE by adding them together, and then rolling 4d6. If you have the **SKILL of CLIMBING** then you can subtract 2 from the roll.

If you pass, turn to **8**
If you fail, turn to **3**

49

The bolt misses the oak beam, and strikes the hard stone wall. It buries itself into the brickwork, but when you tug on it, it just pulls a piece of masonry free. It falls to the ground with a crash.

Add the Codeword **CHISLER**.
You only had the one bolt, and so that option is no longer available to you. Lose 1 **FORTUNE** point

Now you can either:

Use the grappling hook, with a long rope attached. Turn to **48**
Try to get into the gardens behind the house and establish the pattern of the guards.

Turn to **14**

50

As you pull the handle, you stop dead as you notice a very fine wire leading down the left side of the drawer. You lean down, moving your body out of the way so that you can use the silvery gleam of the moon from the window. It's almost impossibly fine. With the edge of your knife you try to cut it – but even the razor sharp steel of the knife can't make an impact. It's incredibly strong. You look even closer and sniff. You recognise the smell. It's vaguely arachnid. It must be the web of the Steelsilk Spider, a rare species famed and prized for their incredibly strong but thin webbing.

The webs from these spiders are expensive – and it makes you want to see the contents of the drawer even more. You search round the desk. There must be a device to disable the trap. After a few seconds searching, you think you have found it. There's a small hole next to the draw but hidden at the back of the desk. You get your finest pick and slip it into the hole and hear a "**THUNK**"

You pull the draw fully open. Inside you find a ledger. You skim through it and see a list of dates, numbers and coded entries. The numbers you assume are prices in gold pieces. The coded entries may relate to clients, goods and addresses. If you decide to keep the **JOURNAL** to examine later, add it to your Adventure Sheet. You also find a purse. You pick it up and shake it.

Roll 1d6 and times that by 10 – that is the amount of gold pieces you find in it when you open it. You put this in your bag. At least you have something to show for tonight's work.

Also there is a vial of clear glass. You hold it up to the limited light and it appears to be a blue green liquid. There is a maker's mark on the bottle and a rune. You open it and the odour makes you queasy and drowsy. You quickly replace the stopper, but it's too late. Your eyes get heavy, and you start to feel sleepy. You nod off briefly, and sleep for about 10 minutes, but then you awaken. You were fortunate you didn't inhale more!

You have found a **POTION OF SLEEP**, which can either be inhaled or drunk. Add it to your Adventure Sheet.

There's nothing further of interest and so you quietly close the drawer and reset the trap by removing your pick. You head for the door.

Write down the Codeword **MOONLIGHTER**

Turn to **40**

51

You leave the room and turn left, and find yourself in front of the door to the other room. Your common sense screams at you not to open the door, but to leave the house as quickly as you can. However, you have always had an overdeveloped sense of curiosity, and you can't help yourself from reaching for the door handle

You curse yourself, thinking one of these days your curiosity will be the death of you. You hope today isn't that day.

You slowly turn the handle.

Turn to **88**

52

On the bed, Malombr starts to moan in pain as his consciousness returns. He murmurs something, delirious in agony. You go over and assess his wounds. Given time, he may recover, as most of the injuries are superficial, but painful. The Raven was careful not to administer any mortal wounds.

You grab the thick grease like ointment from the table, and spread it on his wounds that are still bleeding. You tell his to keep applying this, as it stops the bleeding. You also find a liquid for the pain, and give it to him. He starts to relax a bit but then passes out. You leave him sleeping.

If you have the Codeword **CAT**, you can also use some of the ointment on your shoulder, and this will alleviate your pain. You can increase your **FIGHTING SKILL** and **AGILITY** by 1 each.

You quickly search the room, and check the compartment that opened when you lit the Hand. Inside is something small and disc shaped, and wrapped in silk, and you place it in your bag. Well, you are a thief after all.

You decide it's time to leave the house, in case the Watch were alerted by the screaming. You decide to leave by the front door. However, you don't notice a dark figure hiding in the shadows outside the window, which sees you leave the room. The figure slips into the room and starts to search it. It's eyes, the only part of its face visible due to a black hood and mask, narrow in frustration.

It climbs out for the window, and onto the roof, and keeping in the shadows, passing unseen. There it sits, waiting for you to leave the house, so that it can follow.

Write down the Codeword **FALCON**
Turn to **199**

53

You hear a noise, and turn to investigate it. But then you feel a sharp pain across your back. Sharp claws cut through your tunic. Lose 3 **ENDURANCE** points.

Write down the Codeword **FENCE**

You turn back and see a dark shape in front of you, hissing. It's like a shadow in the dark, with ears like pointed horns on the top of its head. Its red eyes glare at you and its sharp teeth glint even in the darkness.

Yo

u recognize it as a Dusk Devil. It has a long tail, forked at the end, and each of its four legs ends with feet that have long curved claws. You have seen them before on the rooftops of Laeveni, and they normally avoid confrontations. However, you seem to have found its lair. It will fight to the death to protect its home.

DUSK DEVIL   **FIGHTING SKILL 10**
ENDURANCE 9

If you win, turn to **4**
If you lose, turn to **182**

54

Before you enter, you remember the hand in your backpack. You carefully and quietly remove it and read the parchment it came with.

The parchment says that it is a Hand of Glory. It's the left hand of a murderer, who has been hanged. The fat from his body was rendered down to make the candle, and the hair from his head was used for the wick. If you light the candle, it has several uses.

You see a lit candle nearby and move to light the Hand. The assassin hears the sound of you move and turns quickly. His sword whistles out of his back sheath with almost preternatural speed.

However you have managed to light the flame. As he closes the distance to you, you read out the words on the parchment. The Raven leaps towards you, his sword raised above his head.

"Now open, lock!
To the Dead Man's knock!
Fly, bolt, and bar, and band!
Nor move, nor swerve,
Joint, muscle, or nerve,
At the spell of the Dead Man's hand!"

Two things happen. Firstly the Raven freezes in midair, and Malombr stops squirming in pain. Secondly, there is a "**CLICK**" in the room, and you see a hidden compartment has opened in the oak footboard of the large bed. You ignore that for now, and focus on the Raven. You walk over to him and prod him. He doesn't move, not even blink. He's frozen in time.

You move over to Malombr, and place the Hand of Glory on the desk, next to the Raven's cruel instruments. You walk over to Malombr, and manage to lift him down from the chandelier. He's as stiff as a corpse as you move him. It seems as if all his muscles are frozen. You lay him on the bed.

You hear a spluttering sound, and you turn and see that the candle in the Hand has burnt down very quickly, and now there is just a puddle of wax, and a short wick. The wick starts to get covered with the liquid wax, and the flame will soon be snuffed out.

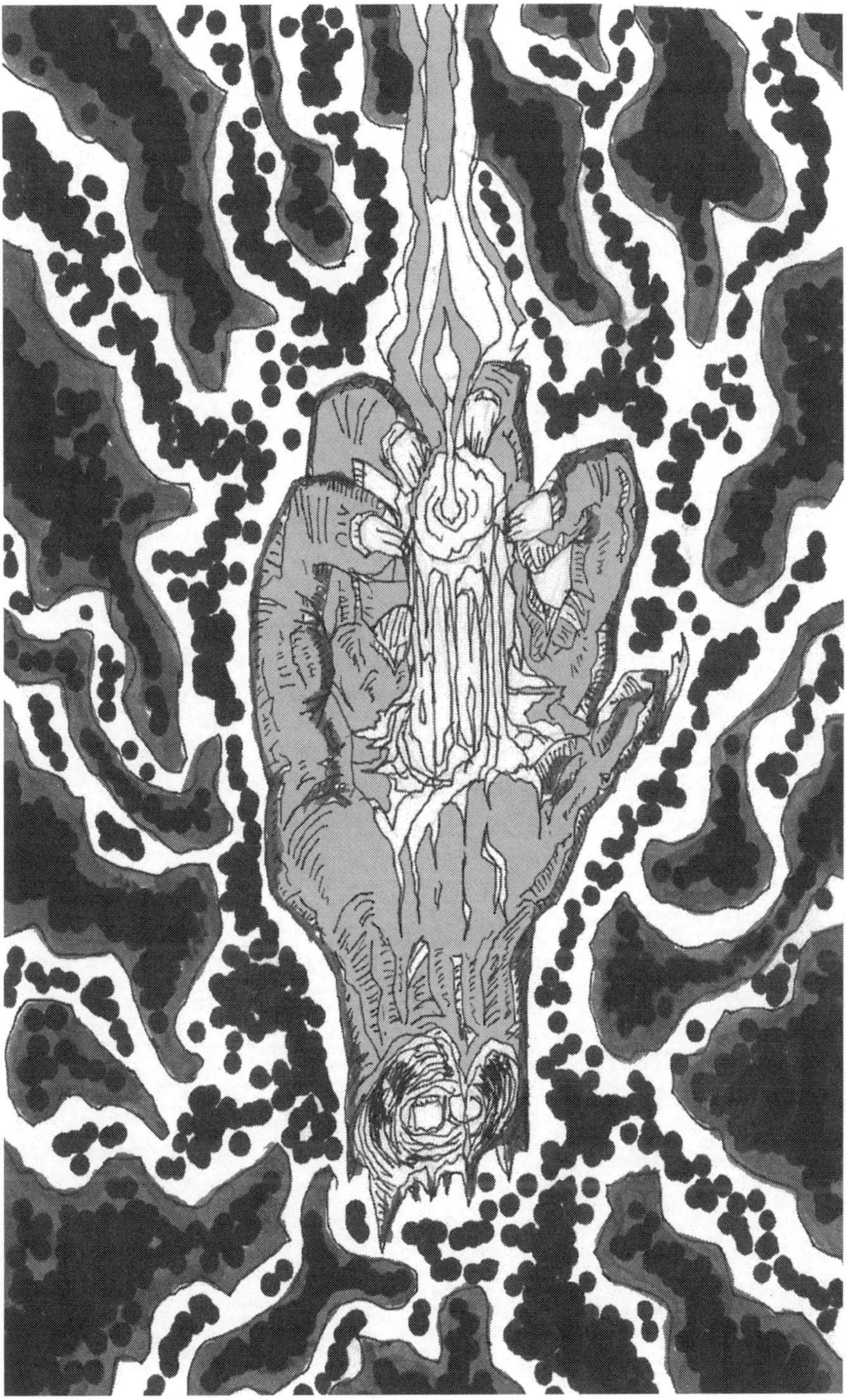

You must act.

You dash across the room with your sword, and see that the assassin is still in midair. You intentionally run him through. No blood spills from the body, no cry from the Ravens shrouded lips. You pull your blade out of the assassin. Then the candles splutters its last, and the assassin crumples to the floor, blood streaming from the chest wound. He groans once, and then dies

Lose 2 **FORTUNE** points for deliberately murdering a person, as cold blooded murder is well known to bring ill luck.

Remove the Codeword **FINGER** from your Adventure Sheet.

Turn to **52**

55

You tell her your name is Jacs, after your best friend, who is currently working elsewhere (you hope). You are pretty sure she won't have heard of a street rat thief such as Jacs.

"Pleased to make your acquaintance. An honest name for an honest man.", she says, half smiling

She stands up, saying,

"My round, I think"

Before you can object, she heads to the bar. When she returns, she has two equally full crystal glasses of whisky. She places them next to each other on the table. Both look identical.

"After you", she says, inclining her head.

Are you going to take the glass on your left, then turn to **31**
Or the glass on your right, turn to **16**
Or create a diversion, turn to **7**

56

Too shocked by the noise, you fall. You hit the ground below with a thump. Lose 4 **ENDURANCE** points

Gain the Codeword **GRAFTER**

You have no choice but to try entering by the garden. Turn to **14**

57

The lock gives just as Angra comes around the corner. Do you get through the door in time before he sees you?
TEST YOUR FORTUNE
If you have the **SKILL of HIDING IN SHADOWS**, you can reduce the roll by one.

If you pass, turn to **80**
If you fail, turn to **5**

58

The One Eyed Rat is well-placed. As it's one of the larger establishments near the harbour front, it's very close to a main entrance of the sewers. You quickly find the entrance and pull up the metal cover. The smell of refuse, rotting food and worse hits you. It's as mothers milk to you, having spent as nearly as much time in the sewers as you have on the roofs.

Embedded in the walls of the tunnel down are metal rungs. You swing gracefully into the shaft, and start your descent. You reach the bottom, and enter quietly into the knee high water in the tunnel below.

Write down the Codeword **CROCODILE.**

You start to walk east towards the entrance to one of the Jackdaw's hideaways. Its pitch dark in the tunnel. There's no daylight to make its way down from the street at this time of night, and a naked flame is a bad idea in here – due to the buildup of various gases. However you walk confidently, as you know the way well.

Soon you are at a larger junction where the thin tunnel opens up into a large crossroads. You know it's about five yards wide and you wade into the centre. You stop briefly, and it's just as well you do, as then you feel a ripple of the dark water hit your knee. It can't be you, and it's too large a disturbance to be a rat.

The only inescapable conclusion is that someone's in the sewers with you!

Turn to **75**

59

The room is full of shelves. They reach up to the ceiling and on all sides of the room, even around the single window. You feel compelled to enter and search the room.

If you have the Codeword **SOOT**, turn to **97**
If you don't, turn to **30**

60

Not wishing to undergo the same terrifying ordeal of a fight to the death in the dark, you decide to leave the sewer. You find the nearest exit, and climb up the metal rungs back to the street.

The streets are still busy with revelers and drunkards. Ravens are known to hide in plain sight, and kill in crowds using more subtle means such as poison, and so you decide to take to the rooftops.

You jump up and catch the roof overhand and smoothly pull yourself up. You scamper up the side of a house onto the rooftops and stop and look around, crouching down. You start to head inwards, further into the city away from the docks. If other Ravens are chasing you, then you want to distance yourself from your normal haunts. A predictable thief is a dead thief.

You get to the edge of a row of houses, and can either turn left or right.

Write down the Codeword **LIFTER**

If you decide to turn left, turn to **142**
If you want to go right, turn to **130**

61

Part way through the fight. You start to feel dizzy. You stagger, and lower your blade, and get hit by your opponent. Lose 2 **ENDURANCE** points.

You feel like you have been drugged, or poisoned. You manage to regain focus, but you still feel groggy and slow. Lose 1 **FIGHTING SKILL**.

Rub out the Codeword **FENCE** and replace it with the Codeword **CORSAIR**
Turn back to your previous reference and continue the fight.

62

There's a large splash, as your opponent falls dead into the water. You move towards the body, which you find floating a few feet away. Using your touch, you feel the gauzelike mask that's covering the assassins face. It was definitely a Raven. For some reason, the Kindness have marked you for death.

Write down the Codeword **CROCODILE.**

You can either return back to the surface or head onto the rooftops, turn to **60**
Or you can continue to the Jackdaw safe-house, turn to **156**

63

You start to fall, but you manage to grab hold of the line with your left hand. It hurts like hell, but you manage to hang on. However lose 2 **ENDURANCE**, but if you have the Codeword **CAT**, instead lose 4 **ENDURANCE** as you wrench the same shoulder.

You climb back up onto the rope, and crouch down there to regain your strength.
You manage to make the rest of the way over, hanging below the line, hand over hand.

Turn to **69**

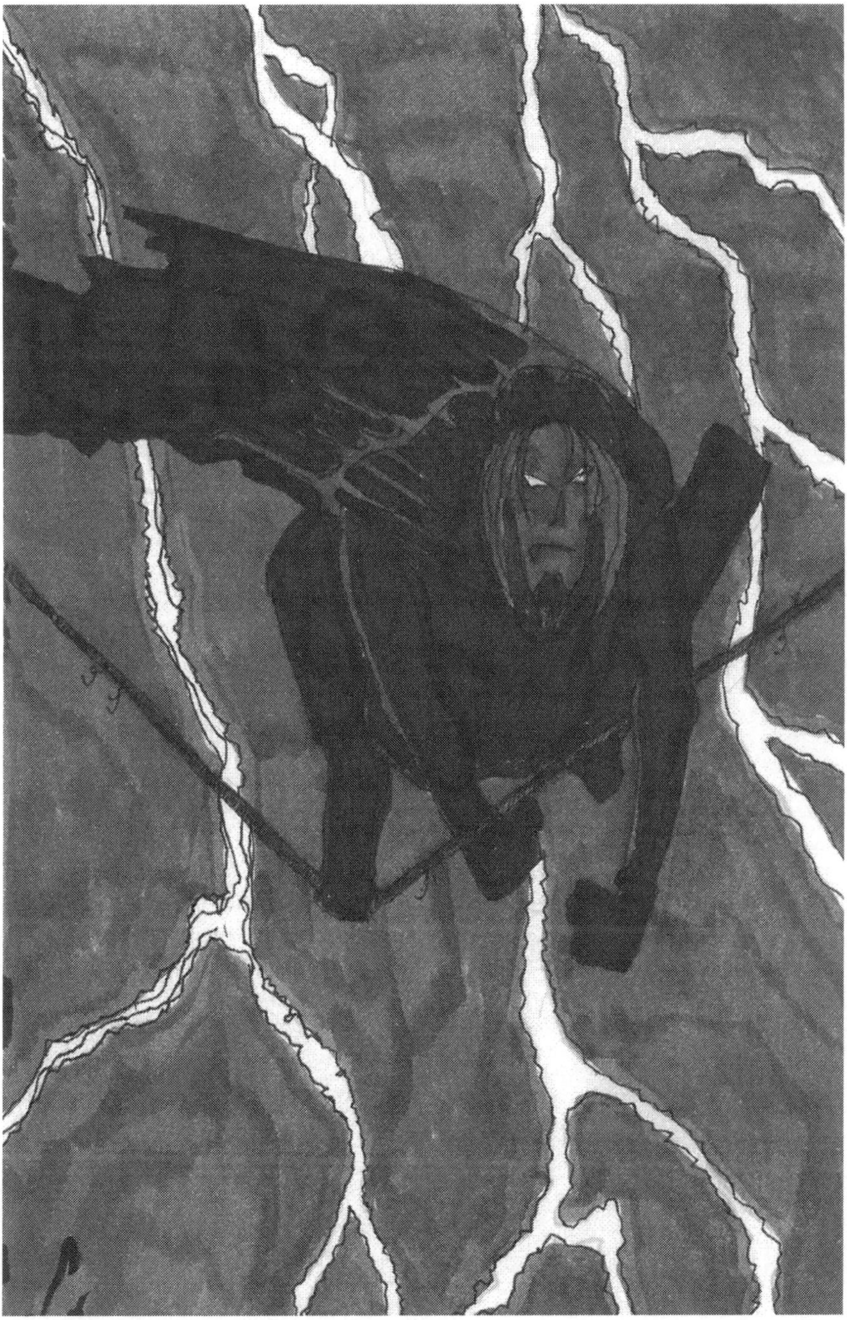

64

You can hear a kerfuffle as you leave the tavern. Apparently the lady is holding her own, as you hear a scream, and it sounds like Brado. You laugh to yourself.

You wonder what to do with the rest of the evening, now your plans have been disrupted. Then you feel a sting in your neck. Damned mozzies. Always bad by the harbour. But then you fall forward, to the hard cobbled floor.

You hear a female voice talking over you,

"He clearly did not have it. Return to the merchant's house and tear it apart. I want it back. Tonight. No matter the cost."

"*Yes, dread lady*", replies a deep voice.

TONIGHT WAS YOUR LAST ADVENTURE

65

You reach inside your pocket, and pull out the silk wrapped item. It feels hot to the touch, unusually, and you hold it out. Lilith smiles widely, and reaches out and takes hold of the item.

"*Finally*", grinning with pleasure. **"And now your reward, as agreed. As much gold as a man will ever need."**

She reaches into a bag slung over her shoulder. It looks heavy, and you hope it contains as much gold as you can imagine. She pulls out a small dagger, and flicks it at you. It turns end over end, and thuds into your neck.

"But then again, a dead man needs no gold," she smiles, **"And thank you for your service, Shadow. Maybe one day we will meet again in my mother's realm."** Then she laughs, and turns and leaps off the roof and disappears into the night.

The nerve poison is fortunately quick. Your body topples off the roof, and falls to the street outside the One Eyed Rat. Lecas hears the noise and rushes out and sighs, sadly.

66

If you have the Codeword **CROOK**, turn to **47** now
Otherwise, read on,

After surviving the seemingly unprovoked attack in the alley, you decide it's not safe on the streets.

What do you want to do now? You must decide.

If you have the Codeword **CROCODILE**, turn to **60**
If you have the Codeword **LIFTER**, turn to **58**

If you don't have either, you can:
Go into the sewers, turn to **58**
Try the rooftops, turn to **60**

67

This time it works. The rung breaks, and Seth's foot drops down. The sudden change of weight means that Seth loses his grip on the ladder. He falls backwards. Falling to his death. He lands with a thud, some distance below.

Enoch hears the scream of his friend, and looks down from the rooftop. You climb up, safely.

"What happened? What did you do to Seth?"

"Me, nothing.", you reply earnestly. *"It looks like the ladder gave way. Look, the rung down there is broken. The salt air of the harbour rots wood quickly."*

Enoch scowls at you, seemingly his favorite expression.

If you have the **SKILL OF CHARM AND GUILE**, turn to **104**
If not, **TEST ENOCH'S INTELLIGENCE.** He has an **INTELLIGENCE** of 8. If he passes, then turn to **104**
If he fails, turn to **86**

68

Almost as soon as you start fighting, you start to feel increasingly groggy and sick. Your hands start to shake, and you sweat profusely – more than you should from the fight alone. You vision becomes blurred, and you feel as weak as a kitten.

Lose 1 **FIGHTING SKILL** and **2 ENDURANCE**
If you survive the fight, replace the Codeword **CORSAIR** with the Codeword **CROOK**

If you are still alive, turn to your previous reference and conclude the fight

69

Despite the rain, you reach the wooden beam of the house, and pull yourself up into the roof. You leave the wire still attached to the beam, in case you need it later. You scamper over the rooftop, to the back of the house, where it is darker, as it's shielded from the street lamps.

You peek over the roof and look down. You can see immediately below there is a small window. It's closed. You decide to try to enter here. You hang from the roof by one hand. Your feet find the narrow ledge and balance on it, and then manage to use your other hand to grab the top of the window. You transfer your weight forward and let go with your top hand, but the sill is slippery with the rain, which has stopped as suddenly as it started.

TEST YOUR FORTUNE. If you have the **SKILL OF SPEED AND AGILITY**, then you can reduce the roll by 2.

If you pass, turn to **89**
If you fail, turn to **82**

70

You pick up the small bundle of fur. In terror, it lashes out with a claw and scratches you. Lose 1 **ENDURANCE** point, but if you had the Codeword **FENCE**, read on. If not, start reading again at *

If you had the Codeword **FENCE**, you can now remove it.
The claws of a Dusk Devil have exude a toxin, which is designed to kill or paralyse smaller animals. With time, the toxin can be dangerous to humans and lead to various side effects. Fortunately, a scratch from a different Dusk Devil neutralises the toxin. That was fortunate. Regain 1 **FORTUNE** point.

*However if you didn't have the Codeword **FENCE**, write it down now.

You look at the small creature. It's only the size of your hand, with spiky yet fluffy dark grey fur with light whiskers. Its yellow eyes are round with a slit for a pupil, and they rarely seem to blink. Its teeth is full of short, sharp little teeth, and it's got a long, thin slightly forked tongue. It looks at you half quizzically, half terrified. It's absolutely adorable.

Adult Dusk Devils are wild, fey creatures, which cannot be trained or tamed. They are not evil, not good, just themselves. They are unpredictable, sometimes shy, and sometimes savage. They are mostly left to their own on the rooftops, as they rarely bother humans (or other similar creatures, except maybe the odd extremely small hobbit), and they feed mainly on rats, pigeons and other vermin.

However, if you can catch a baby, then they are much sort after. They are part magical, and have a great resistance to spells, and can also sense the arcane. Wizards and witches will pay a fortune for a baby Dusk Devil. You think that you can sell it, him or her, but when you look down into its face that goes out of your mind as the creature is delightful.

You raise your other hand and tickle the creature's tummy. It purrs in delight, almost like a cat, and its eyes close into a squint in enjoyment. Then after a while, it starts to nod off to sleep. As it sleeps, it looks like a spiked ball of dark grass. As it grows the fur will darken and you laugh, thinking it will look like a ball of soot, or a-

Soot! You think. The ideal name. You carefully place Soot in a pocket of your tunic. Soot half wakes, and snuggles down and is soon back asleep.

Write down the Codeword **SOOT**.
Turn to **78**

71

You pick up the heavy crossbow, and wind back the string until it clicks into place, held by the trigger. There is about 150 pounds of pressure held coiled in the strained ash limbs. Its hard work to even draw the bow using the winch. You place the metal bolt into the flight groove, and make sure that the attached wire is coiled loosely and without tangles. You take aim at the heavy wooden crossbeam that runs horizontally underneath the eves of the large house. You pull the trigger.

TEST YOUR FIGHTING SKILL. If you pass, turn to **32**
If you fail, turn to **49**

72

It's a tricky climb down, and you are almost there, when you slip. You fall about 5 yards and land heavily on the ground below. Lose **2 ENDURANCE**

Write down the Codeword **GRAFTER**
You have no choice but to try entering by the garden. Turn to **14**

73

Experience has meant that you have kept your body subtle and ready for action whilst waiting. You easily make the leap across the alley, landing lightly on the opposing rooftop, which barely groans with your light weight. You smile to yourself. The last time you had made this jump, you had failed and fallen to the street below. This had led to a chain of events that meant you inadvertently had to save the city, and maybe even the world. Not that those poor souls below remember. All this occurred under that streets in ancient catacombs, where primeval powers had struggled for the very soul of Laeveni. All this flashes through your mind in a matter of seconds.

Malombr moves cautiously through the street. No one has the nerve to get in the way of his hideous guards. You follow him along the rooftops, as quiet as a shadow. As you cross into the merchant's district, you drop back to the ground and follow at street level. You don't need to follow too closely as you know exactly where he is heading – his townhouse.

You slip ahead of him on the rooftops, eager to arrive at his townhouse first. It's a short journey and you easily outpace the merchant and his lumbering guards. You decide to wait in the rooftops and watch.

Malombr crosses the Market Square and moves down Market Street and then turns right. You wait at the junction, as his house is just over the road and you don't want to alert him – now that the streets are quieter. You listen and hear as he unlocks the door and it creaks open. A few moments later it shuts, and you can hear a number of locks being engaged. You know from watching that the front door is tough to crack – as it is now locked internally when the master is in residence. But you have other routes planned.

You watch as the large bodyguards start to patrol the borders of the house. They will do so until dawn, when the master awakens. You laugh to yourself. The Shadow of a year ago may have approached from street level. Then it is likely that your corpse would be hanging disemboweled from a nearby street lamp - a free meal for any local scavengers.

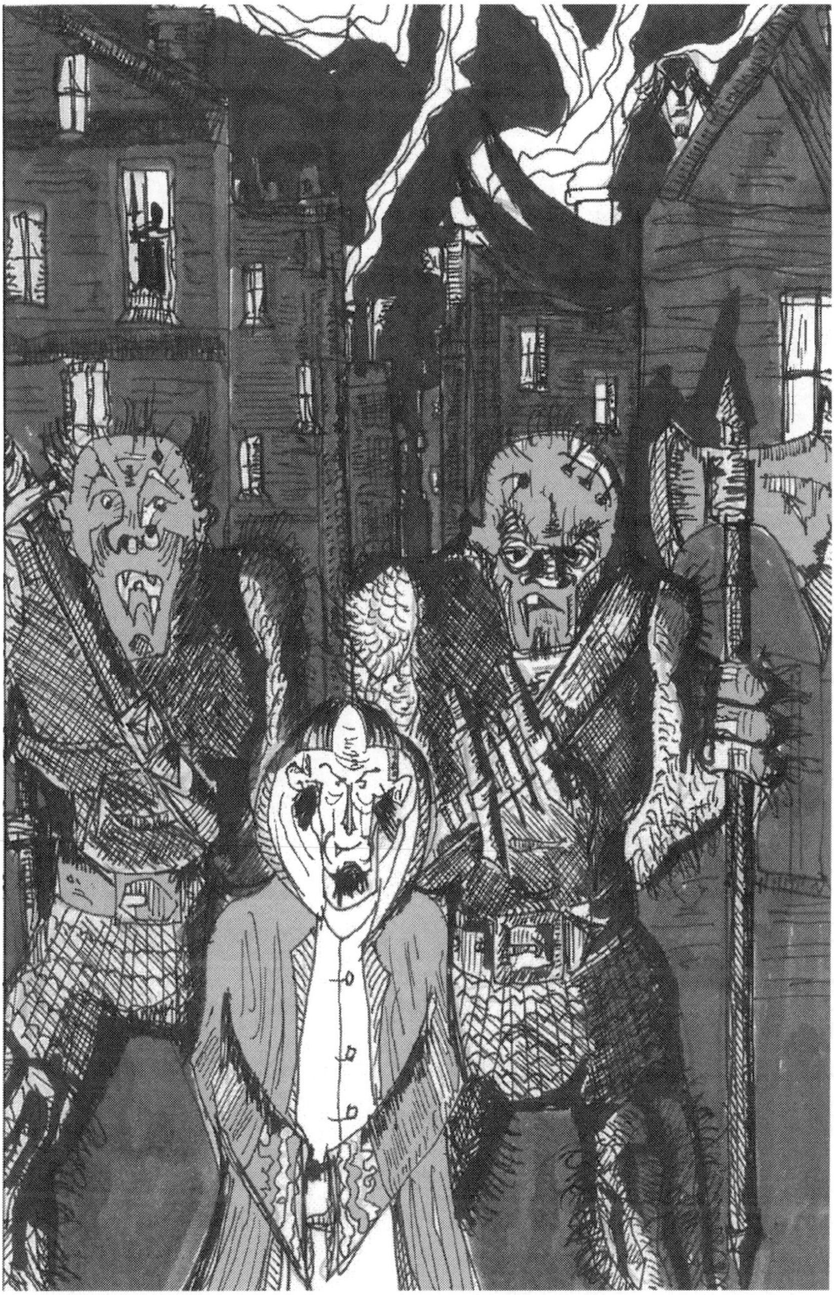

However, now you are a Master Thief. After the "incident" a year ago, you have slowly re-built the Thieves Guild, which you have named as the Jackdaws, after the dark birds that have a penchant for stealing shiny objects. You are now the Guild Master, the youngest in history, with your good friend Jacs as your deputy. The Jackdaws are still small, compared to the Guilds previous size and strength, but thriving.

You have always felt you had unfinished business with the merchant Malombr, as you were about to rob him a year ago. Since then, his wealth has grown, and there were rumours that he imported some goods that had dark aspects, and evil uses. Despite being a thief, you have a strong sense of ethics and right and wrong. You try not to steal from honest folk, especially those who have little themselves. And you have a deep hatred of the arcane and black magic. Anyone who aligns themselves with dark powers deserves to be robbed.

You bring yourself back into the present. You should know better than to reflect, philosophise or contemplate when you are working. You need to focus on the job, and only the job.

This is as far as you have got so far. You have never been inside the house. In fact, you have never got further than the very rooftop you are perched on. The house is grand, and set in its own grounds, meaning there is no direct access from roof to roof as the distance is too far to jump. You will need to find another way.

You have devised three possible options. Hidden on the rooftop in a chimney are various items you secreted there last night.

Do you want to try to:
Use the crossbow with a heavy barbed bolt, which has a sturdy wire attached to it. Turn to **71**
Use the grappling hook, with a long rope attached. Turn to **48**
Or, do you want to try to get into the gardens behind the house and establish the pattern of the guards. Turn to **14**

74

If you have the Codeword **FALCON**, turn to **123**
If not, turn to **178**

75

After a minute or so of staying still, you still haven't felt or heard anything else to indicate and intruder. But you know, you just know in the marrow of your bones, that someone is here. There are few that can match you for moving silently in water, but whoever is in here is equally as skilled as you. Your street logic leads you to two possible conclusions.

Either another jackdaw is down here, but you dismiss that as they are all assigned elsewhere tonight. Another bird hunts. A Raven.

To run would be suicidal. You would not know which way to go and may run into a black lacquered blade. You could also trip over and that would be just as bad. As slow as you dare, you draw your sword. It makes no sound as you inch it out of its scabbard.

You stand there, and close your eyes. They will be just a distraction. You reach out with your senses. You enemy could be on any side of you, but you cannot just wait for them to find you. You must act. You sense they are close, but which way do you strike?

FIGHT IN THE DARK

The chart below shows you in the centre (S). You can choose to strike in one of the areas numbered 1 to 8. If you get the number exactly right, then you hit your opponent, and do 4 **ENDURANCE** points damage. If you get the number either side, then you wound them with a glancing blow, and so do 2 **ENDURANCE** damage.

For example, if you choose 3, and you find out your opponent was in area 3, you do 4 **ENDURANCE** damage to your opponent. If you chose 2 or 5, then you do 2 **ENDURANCE** damage.

The shaded squares illustrate this. Ignore the colours when fighting for real.

1	2	3
4	S	5
6	7	8

You opponent has an **ENDURANCE** of **10**. You must get them to 0 to survive.
Make your decision.
Roll 1d8. Whichever number you roll is where your opponent is.
If you guessed correctly, you hear a groan. Subtract the correct **ENDURANCE**.

However, if you are wrong, and miss, you have telegraphed your current location.
Work out how many **ENDURANCE** points you have lost, using the below table

Look at the number you choose. If the number you opponent was in was two numbers away, then you lose 2 **ENDURANCE**
If it was 3 numbers away, you lose 4 **ENDURANCE**
If your choice was 4 places away, then you opponent is directly behind you and can run you through with a killing blow

So if you chose position 3, and your opponent was at:

Position 1 or 8, you lose 2 **ENDURANCE**
Position 4 or 7, you lose 4 **ENDURANCE**
Position 6, then your opponent is directly behind you. You are killed.
The shaded squares illustrate this. Ignore the colours when fighting for real.

1	2	3
4	S	5
6	7	8

Continue until one of you is dead.
If you win, turn to **62**

76

You are about to pick up the glass to your right, when Soot pops out of your pocket. You had almost forgotten about it. The little creature jumps on the table, and sticks its head half in your glass. It slurps away, until all the whisky has gone.

Soot turns around and staggers a bit, and purrs in pleasure, and you scoop Soot up and put it back in your pocket. You look embarrassed, whereas Lilith looks a bit annoyed.

"Anyway, I must be away. It was a pleasure talking to you.", she says, and stands and leaves. It was a strange encounter that leaves you somewhat perplexed. You cannot decide if you are sad that she's left, or relieved.

Turn to **91**

77

As the guard passes, you manage to hide behind one of the statues. This one is of the merchant himself, rather tastelessly holding a set of scales in one hand, and a pouch of gold in the other. You almost laugh at Malombr. Such efforts he makes with his security, but his vanity means that he had to have statues of himself in the garden. A perfect place for thieves and other miscreants to hide behind.

The guard disappears out of sight. You move again, heading for the back door. You arrive without incident, and kneel down and examine the lock. You pull your picks and go to work.

TEST YOUR INTELLIGENCE. If you have the **SKILL OF LOCK PICKING** you can take 1 off the roll.
Each attempt to pick the lock takes 10 seconds. If you can do it in one or two attempts, turn to **80**
If it takes you three attempts, turn to **57**
If you still haven't picked it after three attempts, turn to **5**

78

You leave the room and find yourself on a landing. There are no more doors on it, and just a wooden stair down. You stand still, listening. The noise of your fight has obviously not alerted anyone. You creep down the stairs, which curve around to the left, silent as a ghost. You find yourself on

You are faced with three choices on this level. Ahead of you, at the far end of this landing, more stairs continue on downward, turning to the right at they descend. Otherwise, there are two doors on the right wall. The first door is painted black, and the second is painted white.

You can now:
Take the stairs, turn to **154**
Try the black door, turn to **59**
Try the white door, turn to **88**

79

It's been a long night, and you are not sure it's one that was well spent. Your tangle with a Raven has left you felling nervous and edgy. You decide to head to the Rat for a drink, and to talk to your friend Lecas. He often has a good handle on what was happening on (and above) the streets.

You walk through the streets, which are busy as its now well after nightfall. All the usual scum come out at night. Robbers, drunks, card sharps, press-men, rogues, prostitutes. You normally feel right at home. But not now. You still cannot lose the feeling that you are about to get a poison dart between the shoulders.

Taking time, you sneak to one of your safe-houses, this one in the attic of a local bakery, run by Leff Rawls. You deposit anything you have stolen this evening. Then you change out of your work gear, and put on a more informal outfit, and leave.

You get to the Rat and walk to the bar. It's busy, but fairly orderly for the port area. Lecas doesn't put up with any bother, and his beer is about the best in town.

You walk up to the bar, and Lecas is busy in conversation with a couple of dwarves at the other end of the bar counter. He sees you and nods and walks towards you. You order a pint of Goblin Basher. Lecas doesn't ask for money. By now you have a tab at the tavern.

"How goes tonight, young master", he asks conversationally. He never uses you name in public anymore.

"Not so good, Lecas. Have you heard any news about my cousins?" you ask.

His eyes narrow. *"Your rather large cousins?"*

You nod. He looks troubled. He whispers, whilst trying to keep his face neutral now,

"I have heard rumours they have lost someone, or something, and were doing everything to find it."

Turn to **37**

80

You slip through the door undetected. You are in a kitchen. For such a grand house, it's a bit pokey. A half empty plate is left on the table, showing a meagre meal of bubble and squeak. For a man of means, Malombr's diet seems very frugal.

You have a quick search and find enough food for three meals, but nothing else of interest.

You creep through the room and find yourself in a hallway. There are a set of stairs to your right. First you see another door off to the left. You decide to try that first.

Turn to **99**

81

Moving to the left, you perch on the window sill. You hook the rope over the arch of the window so it's held in place, in case you need it. You cling to the window like a spider to a wall. On your left hand, there is a silver ring, with a black stone carved in the shape of a jackdaw. It's the symbol of your status, but also has a practical use.

You ball your left hand into a fist, and place the tip of the stone against the leaded window glass. You draw a large circle in the pane. The expensive and rare black diamond scores the glass easily. When the circle is complete, you gently tap on the left side, inside the circumference of the circle. The glass starts to come free, and as you hoped, it pivots vertically, so that the right side of the glass edges outwards. You carefully tease it out and then grab it quickly. With almost no noise, the circle of glass comes free in your hand.

You look behind you, and see a thick hedge in the grounds beneath. With a quick flick of your wrist, you hurl the glass disc into the hedge. It lands with a slight rustle of leaves. You reach inside, and find the latch, and then pull the sash window upwards. The curtains are drawn but you can see feint light from the room inside. Then you hear a scream, a bloodcurdling scream of pain and agony. It's coming from inside the room.

The scream startles you and you start to fall backwards.

TEST YOUR AGILITY. If you pass, turn to **84**
If you fail, turn to **56**

82

As you release your hand, then your balance still hasn't fully transferred across. You start to fall, and try to grab at the window sill. You manage to grab the sill with your left hand, but your shoulder burns with pain as you wrench it badly. **LOSE 2 ENDURANCE**.

You hang there, breathing heavily, your shoulder aching. Your fingers dig into the wet sill, trying to find purchase in the hard wood. You flail around, swinging in the cold night air.

TEST YOUR FITNESS. If you pass, turn to **15**
If you fail, turn to **23**

83

You notice that the dust on the floor has been disturbed by what looks like clawed feet. Then you feel a presence in the room. You reach for your short sword and draw it.

All of a sudden, a dark shape rears up in front of you. It is like a shadow in the room, with ears like pointed horns on the top of its head. Its red eyes glare at you and its sharp teeth glint even in the darkness.

You recognize it as a Dusk Devil. It has a long tail, forked at the end, and each of its four legs ends with feet that have long curved claws. You have seen them before on the rooftops of Laeveni, and normally they will avoid humans. However, you seem to have found its lair. It will fight to the death to protect it's home.

DUSK DEVIL   **FIGHTING SKILL 10**
                                             ENDURANCE 9

If you win, turn to **4**
If you lose, turn to **182**

84

You manage to regain your balance, and hang onto the windowsill. You feel unsure about entering the room.

If you decide against it, you think you can climb down safely, and try entering via the rear garden. Otherwise you will have to steel yourself and go through the window

If you decide to climb down, turn to **72**
If you enter the room, turn to **45**

85

"Ah, Shadow, I was quite fond of you. I had hoped it would not come to this. But as you wish."

Lilith gestures. Enoch walks to a table and unfurls a leather roll to reveal two dozen glinting metal items, each in its own pocket in the roll. There are knives, saws, pliers and some items that you cannot even imagine their uses.

Seth grabs the back of the chair, and drags it over to the table. He stands behind you, holding you firm in the chair whilst unloosening some of your clothing. Enoch approaches you, a knife gleaming in the candlelight. He smiles at you and starts to cut. You start to scream.

If you have the **SKILL OF RESOLVE**, then turn to **43**

Otherwise,
TONIGHT WAS YOUR LAST ADVENTURE

86

Enoch grabs you by the throat, and drags you to the hatch into the loft.

"You cursed rat," he screams at you, *"Seth was my friend. We made our first kill together when we were 12. We trained together. Lived together. Loved together. And you push him from a rooftop. You will die for this, runt."*

There is no thought in his mind. No consequences of his actions. He lifts you over his head with ease, and throws you from the hatch. You cry out as you fall but soon you are silenced when you meet the hard stones with a thud.

Enoch grunts with satisfaction. But then he calms down and realises his error. Lilith will not be pleased with him unless he finds the item. He grimaces.

It must be in the loft. He searches it for hours and eventually finds a secret panel. Behind it are two levers. He almost smiles. He pulls one of them. A great bag of flour drops from the roof, and crushes him.

Tonight it seems, no one wins.

TONIGHT WAS YOUR LAST ADVENTURE

87

You go to walk through the door. If you have the **SKILL OF SIXTH SENSE**, turn to **92**
If not, turn to **95**

88

The door opens quietly and you peer inside. The room is lit by candles, and you wish it had been in darkness. The merchant Malombr is hanging from a chandelier in the centre of the room. He is naked apart from a loincloth. His hands are tied together and hooked over the chandelier. His feet are also tied with rope. His thin body is slick with blood and sweat.

In front of the merchant, with his back to you, is a figure clad in black. He is wearing tight fitting black hose, and a black tunic. His head is covered with a black hood, but you can see as the man's head turns slightly, that only his eyes can be seen. He has a short sword slung over his back, and a weapons belt at his waist.

He doesn't hear you, as when you opened the door, he had just sliced a piece of flesh from Malombr's torso, eliciting another scream.

You recognized the figure in black, even though you have never seen him before, or one of his type. He's a member of the Kindness, a member of the Guild of Assassins, named as they believe that death by their hand is a kind release from mortal suffering.

However, in your Guild they are known by their nickname: Ravens, after the larger corvidae bird that is a larger cousin to the Jackdaw. They have existed in Laeveni as long as you can remember, a shadowy group that like thieves, live in the nighttime. They are well known for being highly effective killers.

Malombr continues to scream, as the Raven ones again slices into his torso. He has already peeled back most of the skin with his knife, and carved away the subcutaneous fat, and now is working on the muscles and nerve clusters.

On a table in front of him are a series of gruesome tools. Flaying knives, cruel hooks, needles, saws. There are also bottles of potions of different types, and he keeps smearing a white fat like ointment onto Malombr's body. It seems to stop the blood from flowing, so he doesn't bleed to death.

Malombr's head is hanging forward. His bowl cut hair in his eyes. He seems to have passed into unconsciousness. The Raven picks up another bottle, and opens the cork underneath the merchant's nose. His head jerks backwards after he inhales the smelling solution.

"There, there, good merchant. Please don't continue to nod off. We have a long journey to go on together, and it will be much quicker if you are awake", chides the Raven, in an almost kindly voice, as if he was gently telling a child off for not eating their greens. The calmness and friendliness of his voice is all the more chilling.

If you decide to help, turn to **20**
If you decide to leave instead, turn to **25**

89

For a moment, you wobble precariously on the thin ledge, but you quickly regain your balance, and cling to the window like a spider to a wall. On your left hand, there is a silver ring, with a black stone carved in the shape of a jackdaw. It's the symbol of your status, but also have a practical use.

You ball your left hand into a fist, and place the tip of the stone against the leaded window glass. You draw a large circle in the pane. The expensive and rare black diamond scores the glass easily. When the circle is complete, you gently tap on the left side, inside the circumference of the circle. The glass starts to come free, and as you hoped, it pivots vertically, so that the right side of the glass edges outwards. You carefully tease it out and then grab it quickly. With almost no noise, the circle of glass comes free in your hand.

You look behind you, and see a thick hedge in the grounds beneath. With a quick flick of your wrist, you hurl the disc into the hedge. It lands with a slight rustle of leaves. You reach inside, and find the latch, and then pull the sash window upwards. You pause for a moment, and close your eyes. Without vision to distract you, you push out your other senses. You cannot hear any movement inside, or feel anything on your skin to indicate the passage of a person. You can only smell the freshly cut glass, and the oil from the wooden window. Deciding it's safe to proceed, you slip into the room.

Turn to **41**

90

You feel you cannot trust Lilith, and you dare not fight her, so you take another option. You take out the item from your pocket, and hurl it to the street below.

"**NOOOOOOOOO**", cries Lilith. But it lands, and smashes into a thousand pieces on the hard cobbles, just outside the One Eyed Rat.

There's a concussive blast where it lands. The whole of the front of the One Eyed Rat ceases to exist in an instance. Faster than you can take in, the blast expands, rising up from the street, and it knocks you clean off the roof, and strips the flesh from your bones as you fall.

Lilith screams, as her body starts to be ripped apart, "**Shadow, you fool. What have you done?**"

But you cannot hear her, as your body has been ripped to pieces.

TONIGHT WAS YOUR LAST ADVENTURE

91

Lilith gets up and leaves. She glances back at you once, and smiles, and then threads her way through the busy tavern. Not surprisingly, no one bothers her.

You sit there for a few moments, thinking. She obviously knew who you were, and came here to see you. But she seems to have got what she wanted, and left. You are part relieved, part disappointed. You couldn't help but be attracted to her, but she also made you feel uneasy.

You leave it a few more minutes, as you are not sure whether you are at risk. You decide its best to leave via the back entrance. You head to the bar and slip behind it. You nod at Lecas who is used to this by now. You slip into the kitchen and into the yard. You jump lithely over the wall.

If you have the Codeword **FRAUD**, turn to **74**
If not, turn to **155**

92

You are about to leave the room, pushing the door open when you notice some runes on both sides of the door frame, about a foot up. You examine them closely without touching, and the air seems hot between the runes. Taking no chances, you jump over the hot barrier. The air behind you fizzles when you land.

Turn to **51**

93

The orc drops to the floor with a thud. You sneak over, and carefully pull the dart from his neck. You smell it, and recognise the acrid smell as the poison from a Lepunia frog. It's lethal to humans, and only the half-orcs prestigious size had stopped him from falling dead within moments.

You stop dead, and realise you are not alone in the house.

If you want to continue up the stairs, turn to **24**
If you decide this caper is getting too dangerous and go to leave, turn to **186**

94

You have no choice but to try entering by the garden. Turn to **14**

95

You leave the hideaway, and make your way through the sewers to the nearest ladder up. Unseen a dark shadow jumps out behind you, two steel swords swinging. You are too slow, and one of the swords slices through your wrist and then your neck, severing both.

TONIGHT WAS YOUR LAST ADVENTURE

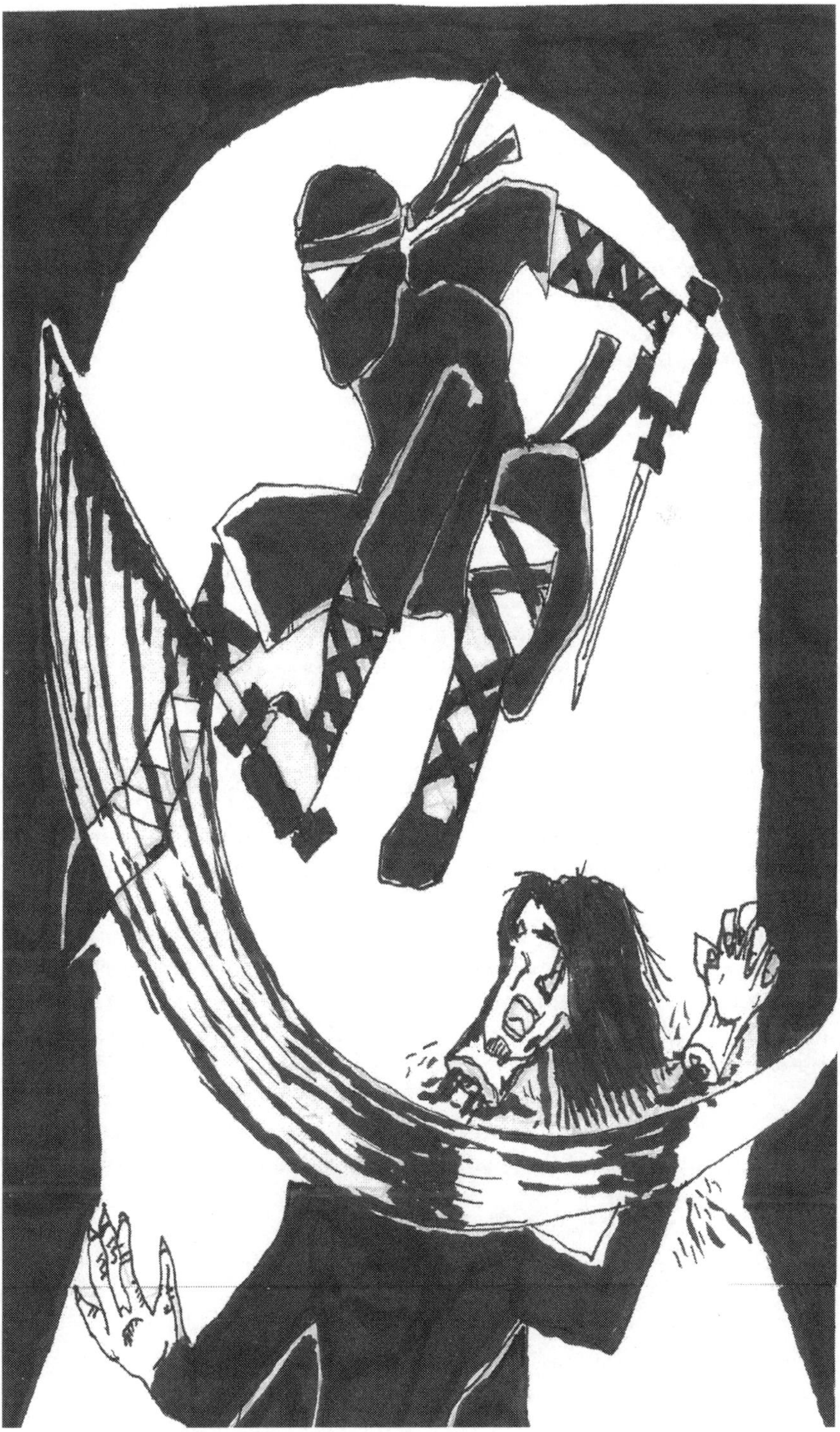

96

If you have the Codeword **GRAFTER**, turn to **5** now

Otherwise read on

The guards have just finished a full patrol and are about to start again. After how many minutes watching do you want to make a run for it across the garden?
1 minute, turn to **5**
2 minutes, turn to **29**
3 minutes, turn to **34**

97

You are about to enter when you hear a little squeal from your pocket, the one that you placed Soot into. You scoop Soot out, and the little creature is very agitated. Its fur it standing on end, and its yellow eyes are wide. It squeals again.

You kneel down and place Soot on the floor. It searches the floor with a snuffling noise, and then its pointed tail swings around and points at a symbol on the door frame. It's very feint, and hard to see even close up, but it's some dark runes, etched into the frame. You cannot read it, but you can sense that there is something emanating from the runes. It seems to cross the doorway at about a foot height and as you place your hand next to it, it's hot. On the opposite doorframe, also about a foot high up, there are the same marks, but this time backwards. It's clearly some sort of arcane trip wire, protecting the room.

You still feel compelled to enter the room and so you pick up Soot, and carefully step over the invisible "*beam*" stretching over the door.

Write down the Codeword **CLIP**

Turn to **12**

98

The wind and rain rushes through your hair as you swing across to the town house. The speed you get to is quite alarming for such a short journey. Then you slam into the wall, the air forced out of your lungs as you impact. Lose 2 **ENDURANCE**.

However, you stop between two windows. One is below you on the first floor or the house, the other is above you. Now you must decide which window to try.

If you want to try the window above you, turn to **81**
If you want to try the window below, turn to **33**

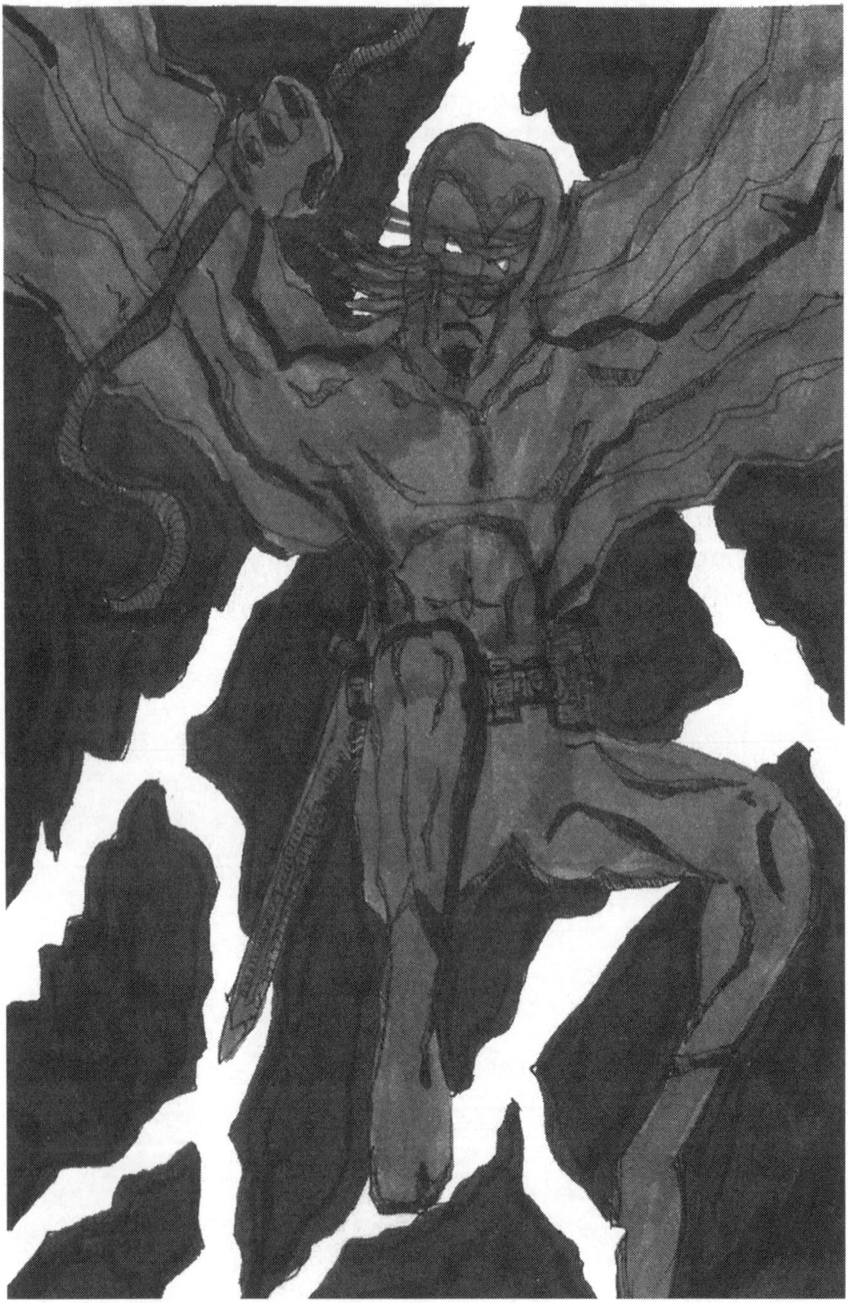

99

You slip through the door like a ghost and find you are in a richly appointed study. There is only one door out of it – the way you entered. In front of you is a desk. There is enough moonlight shining through the window for you to see what's on the desk. There's an inkpot and several quills as well as the wax seal of the merchant. Also there are a number of sheaves of neatly stacked papers. You flick through them but nothing is of interest.

You look at the desk itself. There is a draw in the centre facing you. It's got a small keyhole and you gently move it. It's locked.

Do you want to pick the lock and open the drawer?
If you do, turn to **44**.
If you decide to leave it, then you leave the room and turn to **40**

100

Dawn breaks over the horizon and the harbour starts to be filled with light from the first sun rising. You walk into the Rat, and head to the bar. Lecas is about to finish for the night, with his youngest son taking over. He sees you and waves, looking quite happy to see you. Well, happy for Lecas.

He pulls two pints of Black Breath Ale, and walks over to you. It's the end of your day, so why not. You both sit at an empty table, next to a snoring dwarf, who has had his fill.

"Interesting night?" he asks in a calm voice. Typically understated for Lecas.

"Just a bit. It did not turn out as expected. But in the end I made a tidy profit, I think."

"Well that's the main thing. What next?"

"I don't know, Lecas, I really don't"

"Well, if you are not busy tonight, I hear there is a consignment of silk coming into the wharf on a ship, just after midnight......"

Turn to **200**

101

Somethings not right. That was too easy. They left you still alive, next to the knives, with the ropes binding you loosened. Then all your gear was conveniently in the corner of the room. The room was conveniently unlocked, and there was a conveniently open window.

This all flashes through your mind in moments.

You lean against the wall, pretending to be overcome with the exertions of the night, as you are sure that Enoch, Seth or even Lilith are watching you.

You pant with the effort, leaning over, and carefully looking from side to side, as you seemingly dress the wounds on your body. Sure enough, you spot a dark shape hiding at the back of the alley, and another opposite.

You head to the safe-house where you stored the mysterious object earlier that night, but knowing you are being followed then it is easy to lose them. When you are sure you are not being tailed, you climb up a downpipe onto the roof.

You run across the rooftops and drop into the attic of the local bakery run by Leff Rawls. You recover the item from a hidey hole. You think about opening it. You decide otherwise. You put it inside your jacket.
Turn to **168**

102

The pain is too much for your shoulder.

You lose grip on the ladder, and fall, and land with a thud on top of Seth.

Enoch above hears the noise, and looks out of the attic. He sees you and Seth entangled on the floor, unmoving. Carefully he makes his way down the broken ladder, reaches inside your tunic. He finds the silk package, and walks off without a further look back.

Lilith will be pleased with him. He almost smiles.

TONIGHT WAS YOUR LAST ADVENTURE

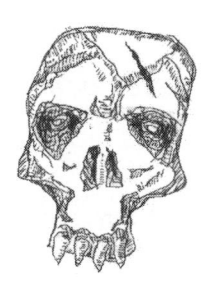

103

You feel you cannot trust Lilith, and you dare not fight her, so you take another option. You take out the item from your pocket, and hurl it into the water below.

"**NOOOOOOOOO**", cries Lilith. But it lands, with a splash, and drops beneath the surface.

She stares at you in disbelief.

"Oh Shadow, you really are quite the one, aren't you", she smiles. **"But I will regain that which is mine"**

"But what is it?" you ask

"Ah, that is really none of your concern. I would suggest you leave it lie where it is. I will recover it, and I would not take kindly to any further meddling."

You decide its best not to disagree.

"I promise, oh lady."

She smiles, and walks over to you, almost effortlessly on the narrow ridge of the roof.

"Shadow, I really am quite fond of you", Lilith says, holding her hand up to your face. *"Tonight has not gone as expected, and many of mine have gone to meet My Mistress early. But, I cannot remember the last time I had so much fun."*

"Then am I not in danger?" you ask, surprised. You were convinced she would kill you.

"Always. A life of a thief is danger, is it not? But not from me. There is no honour in killing without reason, and I have no reason to hurt you now."

She runs her nails over your cheek. You are half enamored, half repulsed.

"But cross me again, boy, and you will see a different side of Lilith." She smiles sharply, and her brown eyes glow golden.

"Now, I have much to do, fare thee well, Shadow"

And with that she drops off the edge of the roof, and disappears into the pre-dawn.

Turn to **100**

104

He grunts, not convinced, but still sticking to his mission. You may not be as fortunate again, as his anger is simmering. He hasn't found the hatch yet, and so you open it, and go to slip into the room.

Enoch puts his arm across you,

"**Me first, rat**." he growls, and he slips through the hatch. You decide to follow.

You are in a dark and dingy loft. There is no window, and the ceiling is low and beamed. There's a brick wall, that's part of the chimney from the bakery below. Despite the early hour, master baker Leff Rawls, is hard at work, as the bricks are warm as the ovens below bake the day's bread.

"Where is it?" demands Enoch.

"Over here", you point and start to lead. You walk to the wall, and pull out a brick, showing two levers.

"I just need to pull these, and the compartment will open." You explain, pointing at the levers *"Or would you rather do it?"*

He looks at you, trying to decide if it's a trap.
"**You do it**", he orders.

You have three choices:
Pull the left lever, then the right, turn to **160**
Pull the right lever, then the left, turn to **161**
Pull both at once, turn to **162**

105

The man in brown drops to the floor. You go over and check him. He's definitely dead. You turn to Enoch, who stands there facing you, his face livid with pure rage and fury. You have made him kill one of his own clan, his own guild.

You cannot resist. You make him drop his sword, which clangs to the floor, bloody. You make him raise his right hand in front of him, palm open. And then quite slowly and deliberately, you raise your right hand, and clasp it to his, shaking his hand.

"Thank you, Enoch. You have been a great help.", you laugh.

If possible, his face grows even angrier, even though he can hardly move a muscle. You really shouldn't taunt him.

He would be a dangerous enemy to leave behind, and you don't know how long the spell from the poppet will hold him. Already, the doll seems to be shrinking, as if the power is being sucked from it.

Are you going to kill him? If so, turn to **111**
If not, turn to **150**

106

You are not quick and nimble enough and get caught in the middle of the throng. You will have to fight another opponent. Once again, roll 1d6

If you get the same opponent, just roll again until you get someone you haven't fought.

Roll	Opponent	Fighting Skill	Endurance
1	Dwarf	8	10

You find yourself in front of a squat but broad dwarf. He has a long, brown beard, indicating he is likely to be relatively young (under 100) and so maybe a bit more impetuous that older dwarves. He is wearing chain mail, over a leather tunic, and slung on his back is a large doubled edge battle axe.

His eyes light up when he sees you,
"Aye, laddie, you do not look like you will last long. A bit of a taster before I find someone truly of worth to tussle with", he grins, *"Rest assured lad, Dewey will rock you to sleep."*

With the he raises a large, gnarled fist, that seems almost the size of your head, and throws a fierce haymaker punch at your head. Can you knock this sturdy dwarf, Dewey, out?
This will be a fight of **ENDURANCE**, and so if you have a **FITNESS** of 10 or over, you can add 1 to your **FIGHTING SKILL**.

2	Barbarian	8	12

You look up and see a huge shadow fall over you. In front of you is a huge barbarian, at least 6 foot 6 tall, clad in furs and scraps of chain mail. She looks down at you and laughs,
"You a scrawny excuse for a man. Sheldra will knock you out with one blow. HA!", she laughs.

You don't doubt her. She is all muscle and long arms and legs. Your only hope is probably speed and agility. If you have the **SKILL OF SPEED AND AGILITY**, you can add 1 to your **FIGHTING SKILL**.

| 3 | Man in Blue | 9 | 13 |

You find yourself faced with the man you saw start the fight, and you realise that it was a distraction to get to you. In every way he's an average looking man. Height, weight, looks. However there's a coldness to his eyes, and he moves with a relaxed litheness. He is dressed in a smart doubled breasted blue tunic, well made, but not so fine that it stands out. He is dressed that he can pretty much fit into any part of Laeveni's society, unremarkable, and instantly forgettable. He wears tall leather boots, and at his waist is a long rapier.

He says nothing, but smiles thinly at you, and then drops down into a wrestling stance, arms outstretched, and then he lunges at you. He is fast, like a striking snake. You will have to be patient. If you have the **SKILL OF FORBEARANCE**, you can add 1 to your **FIGHTING SKILL**

If you win this tussle, write down the Codeword **DESPOILER**.

| 4 | Ogre | 7 | 14 |

You find yourself face to face with an ogre. These creatures are ape like, in their arms are as long as their legs, and they tend to walk on all fours. It's dressed in nothing but a dirty loin cloth, and its body is powerful with a thick torso, a large belly and sagging pectorals. Its legs and arms are long, but thin, but still contain terrible strength.

Ogres are not great conversationalists, but its pig like eyes light up when he (or her) sees you. She (or him) swings a large fist at your head.

Ogres heads are notoriously as thick as the stone they love to burrow into, and so using your brain is your best bet in this fight. If you have an **INTELLIGENCE** of 9 or over, you can increase your **FIGHTING SKILL** by 1.

| 5 | Man in Brown | 7 | 11 |

The man in brown you noticed entering earlier pushes an almost unconscious Halfling out of the way and stands before you. He says nothing, but straight away drops into a fighting stance. He looks well practiced.

You will need a bit of luck to beat this man. If your **FORTUNE** is 9 or over, you can add 1 to your **FIGHTING SKILL**

| 6 | Goblin | 6 | 8 |

The goblin before you is one of the few creatures in the room that you are taller than. It's barely half a foot over 5 feet, and its skinny and scrawny, with a long hooked nose, pointed ears, and large yellow eyes. Its green grey scaly skin is clad in basic leather armour.

However, Goblins are notoriously dishonorable and this one has drawn a short knife, which just fits between his dirty fingers. Any hits from this foe will inflict real damage to your **ENDURANCE**. You do not need to roll 1d6 for the goblin is it hits you, as any strike will inflict 2 **ENDURANCE** points which you will not gain back later.

Remember, your **FIGHTING SKILL** is reduced by **TWO** for this fight. However, if you have the **SKILL OF UNARMED COMBAT**, then it remains at your normal level.

Use the **ENDURANCE** level you were at when you ended the first brawl.

Roll	Blow	Effect
1	Straight punch	1 ENDURANCE
2	Straight kick	2 ENDURANCE
3	Uppercut	3 ENDURANCE
4	Roundhouse punch	4 ENDURANCE
5	Roundhouse kick	5 ENDURANCE
6	Knock Out punch	Knocks out opponent

If you win, you manage to sneak out of the tavern. Write down the Codeword **CON** and turn to **148**

If you lose, you are knocked unconscious, if you have the Codeword **BRIGAND**, turn to **138**
Otherwise, write down the Codeword **LARCENER**, and turn to **129**

107

They do not believe you, and in short order you are taken to a near blockhouse. There, the Sergeant grins as he sees you. You have been in his care before but you managed to escape. There will be no such escape this time. You are stripped, and given a plain white shift to wear and thrown into a cell. Two guards watch you.

There's nothing you can now do. You can see overhead a small barred window in the top of the blockhouse. You watch with creeping horror as the pitch black slowly turns to grey, and then as the dawn breaks through the smog of Laeveni. In your mind's eye you can see the gallows clearly, waiting for you. Your life is now measured in a matter of minutes, not hours.

Shortly the guards open the door. You are bundled into a wagon and driven up into Hangman's Square and you are taken into a holding cell. From the cell there is a window, overlooking the gallows. Already in the cell are five other occupants. Before leaving one of the guards paints a number 7 on your forehead in red paint. You look round and see the other occupants all have the numbers one to six on their heads, and realise what this means.

After only a few moments, but which seems like a lifetime, the guards come and drag number one away. The poor wretch looks terrified, and pleads with the guards. They laugh in his face, and tell him to save his words for God – as he was going before his judgement. He is dragged off, and you can hear the sounds of the crowds cheering as he is brought to the gibbet. Despite the early hour, a public execution was always a popular attraction in Laeveni.

Over the next minutes, numbers two to six each go to the same fate. Each takes it differently. Two struggles violently and is eventually clubbed unconscious. This gets jeers from the crowd when they don't see a good spectacle as he dies still unconscious. Number three stays silent and impassive, having accepted his fate. Number four prays to his pagan gods and is taken outside looking like he is almost at peace. Number five tries bribery, which just results in more laughs from the guards and a bloody nose. Six says nothing.

Then you are by yourself, but not for long, as the guards soon come and take you out into the blinding morning sun. You are half dazzled as you are led up the rough wood steps to the gibbet, where they are just cutting down number sixes still twitching corpse. You are quickly taken and the noose placed over your head. You are not offered a blindfold (the crowd love to see the faces of the condemned as they die), and not allowed anytime to speak.

The Magistrate says a few short words, saying you had been found guilty of attempted larceny. You have been tried in your absence in accordance with the norms of Laeveni. Then the crowd goes silent in anticipation.

The Executioner reaches for the level to open the trap. You can only hope the fall is clean and breaks your neck to kill you instantly. But again fate is playing with you. Due to your sleight frame, the drop is not enough and instead you suffer the pain and indignity of one final dance. The last face you see in this life is of a tall slim woman with raven dark hair. You remember her from the One Eyed Rat. She smiles as she sees you drop.

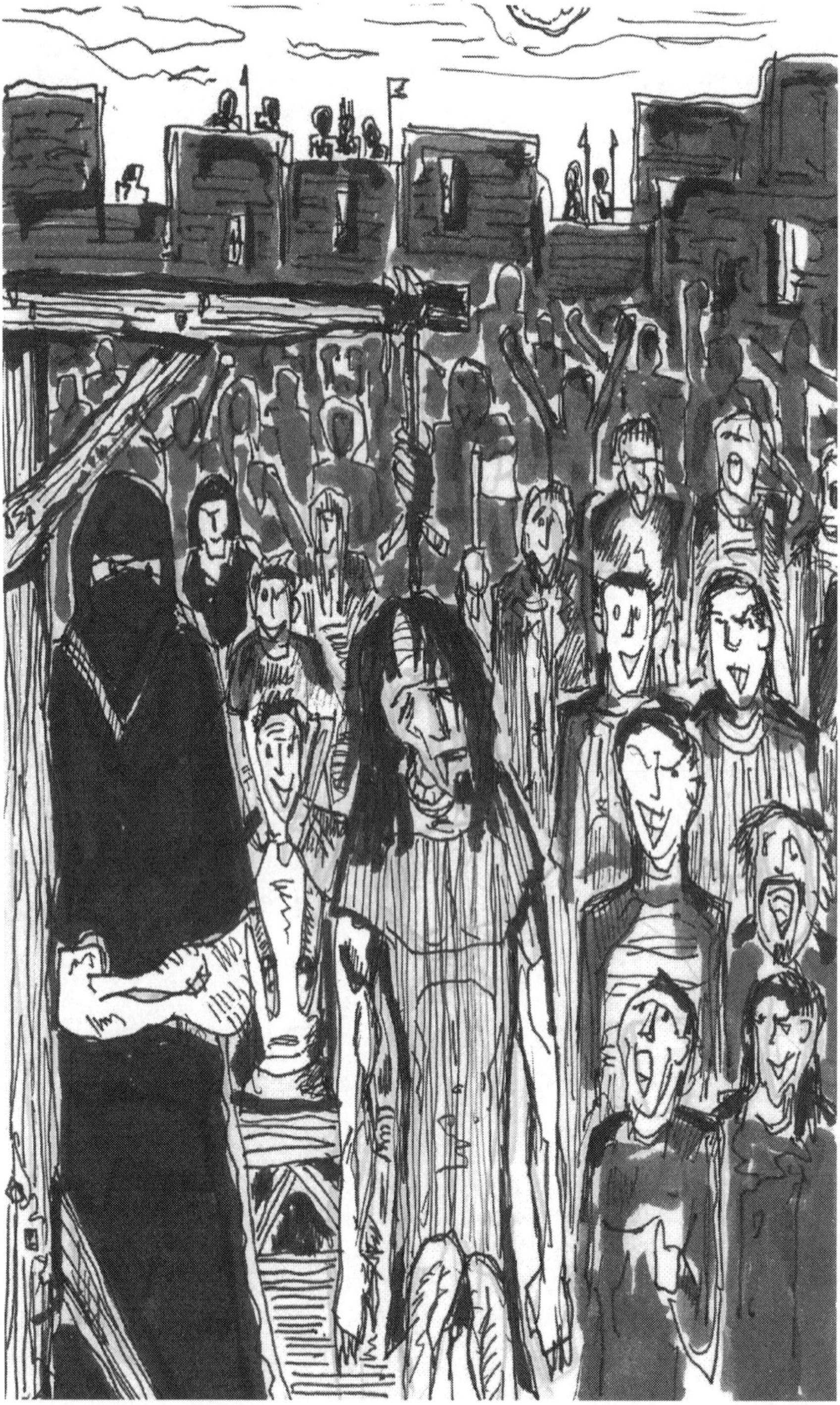

When you finally stop kicking, you are cut down and thrown on a cart with the others. The cart then takes your bodies to a pit outside the city walls, and you are thrown in a mass grave and buried without a marker.

TONIGHT WAS YOUR LAST ADVENTURE

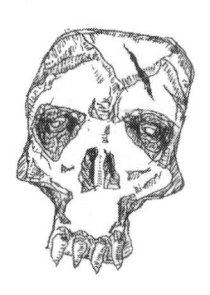

108

You are about to leave, when a man grabs you by the arm. He's just a normal bruiser that frequents the harbour taverns and inns, and known to be muscle for hire. You don't know his name, but you have seen him around.

"Now, laddo, not so fast, there's someone who wants a word with you. It would be most rude of you to leave."

He escorts you over to a table. Sat there is the lady you saw entering the tavern.

You notice that Brado is sat at his table, nursing his arm and glumly sipping his beer. It seems that the lady was able to deal with him without your help.

However, lose 1 **FORTUNE** point, as you feel guilty that you did not help the lady to start with.

The bruiser pushes you into the seat opposite her. The lady nods at the ruffian, who turns and leaves, heading for the door. You have time to further assess her.

She's tall, with raven black hair, cut to her shoulders and it bobs around her face. Her fringe is straight and covers her forehead. She has a wide, pale face, high cheekbones, with warm brown eyes, a long straight nose, and thin lips – that always seen to be turned up in a sardonic half smile.

She is dressed in practical clothes, but of a fine cut. A black leather vest buttoned up over a fine silk shirt that billows over her arms. She is wearing black leather boots that reach mid-calf, and black satin trousers. At her waist is a thin silver handled rapier, and a thin silver dagger, hanging together beside each other.

She raises up her hand, **"I must apologise for asking that ungainly gentleman to escort you to my table, but I did so wish to talk to you."**

She smiles, fully this time. You cannot help but smile as well.

"I am Lilith", she continues, and then pauses, staring expectantly at you.

Are you going to tell her your true name, if so turn to **26**
If you want to say your name is Vostede Mesmo, turn to **42**
If you want to say your name is Jacs, turn to **55**

109

The night must have taken a bit out of you, as when you go to move off, you trip, and fall off the roof when you are still a floor up. You land with a thud, in the street. Lose 2 **ENDURANCE**.

You try to stand up, but find strong arms grab you and haul you to your feet. Two off duty soldiers hold you up.

"Now now, what's this, Erv?" says the first.
"Not so sure Carv, it seems to be raining street rats tonight", laughs the second.
"What do you reckon we should do with him?"
"Well, rightfully, we should take him in, but having just come off duty-"

You start to come to your senses.
"Good gentlemen, thank you for your help. I had to make a rather quick exit from my lady friend's window, and seem to have slipped and fallen"
They look at you suspiciously, but also half curious.
You continue,
"Sadly, my friend's husband returned earlier than expected. He is a marine in the navy, and got to shore sooner than she expected"

You hope you can gain their sympathy, as marines traditionally hate land soldiers, and that hatred is reciprocated.

If you have the **SKILL of CHARM AND GUILE**, turn to **147**
If not, turn to **107**

110

You dodge in a gloomy alley, just in time to see three dark clad figures leap from street to street over the roof above you.

You seem to have thrown them off your scent, for now.

You wait, but the assassins have disappeared into thin air. A few doors away, you can see a tavern, called the Hanging Gate Inn. You decide to take refuge in it for a while, as the rooftops seem too dangerous.

You stumble into the Hanging Gate, and buy a pint of Evil Eye. This costs you 2 gold pieces. You find a small table out of the way, and nurse your pint.

Turn to **136**

111

Leaving an enemy alive is always a bad idea. You do not like killing, despite having to do so far too often, but you resolve not to take the risk. However, you decide to use the poppet to do it. You move

Enoch's free hand to his belt knife. You make him draw it and place the point at his navel.

Enoch looks at you with pure fury, but he cannot do anything to stop you. You move the poppet's arm out a couple of inches. Enoch's arm pulls back so the dagger is a foot away from his body. Then you bring the poppet's arm forward. The knife point moves towards Enoch's stomach, and his eyes widen in fear. But then it stops, an inch before Enoch's flesh. You try to push the poppet's arm through again, but it won't budge.

Then something strange happens. The poppet seems to grow in size, and then you feel power surge up the arm you are holding it in. The button eyes seem to stare at you, and stop you from moving, as if you are being hypnotized.

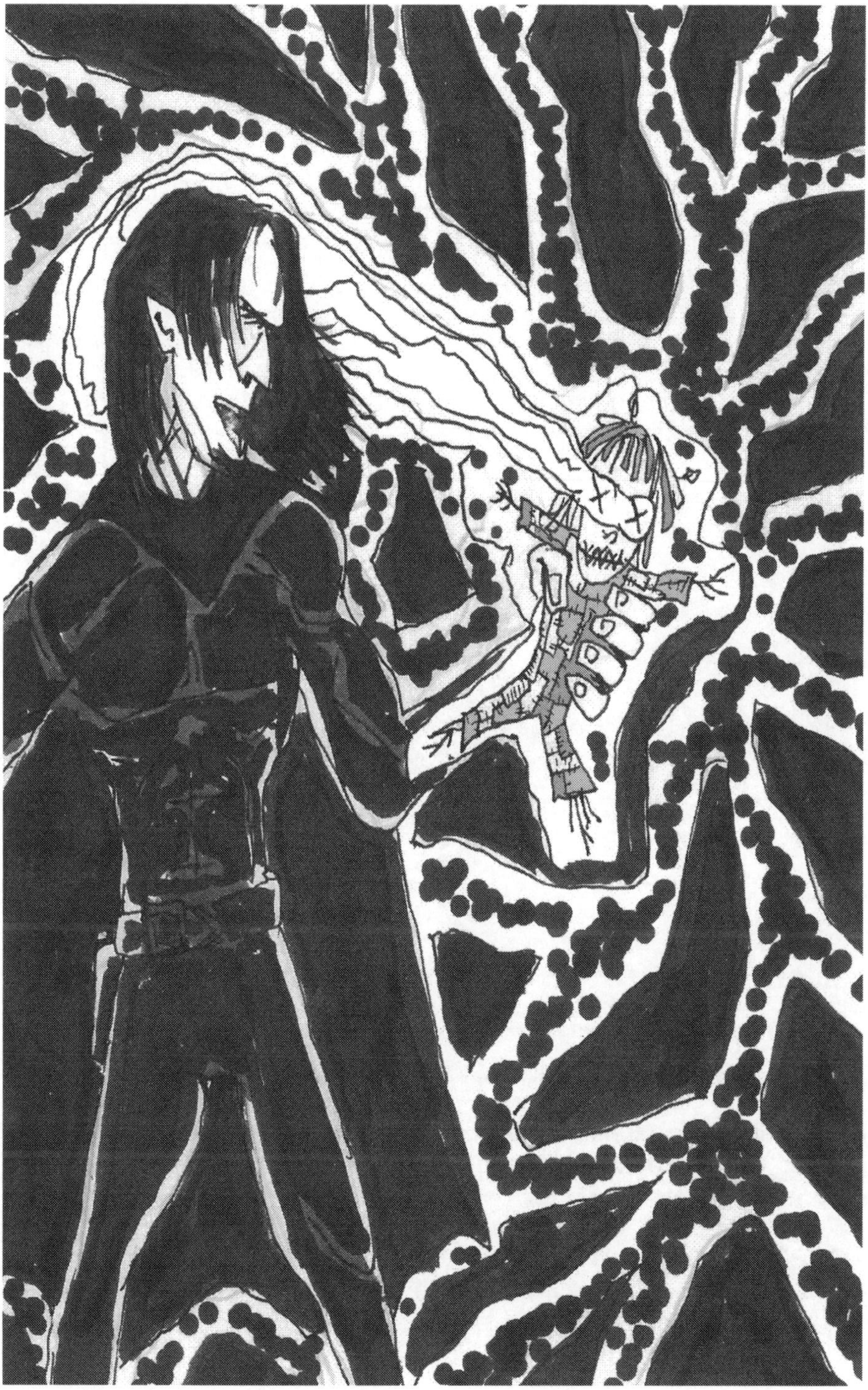

The power throbbing up your arm increases, and your body starts to heat up. You try to drop the poppet but you cannot blink, let alone move a muscle. You start to panic.

Here's the thing. Poppet's are part of fey magic, but they are made for control over a subject, not to kill them. They are not aligned to black magic's, and not made for murder. Normally they were used in love, to control a person who had no interest in you. Immoral and wrong maybe, but never lethal.

As soon as you tried to use the power in the poppet to kill its puppet, then the energy from the doll is released. Enoch is free from his confines. Despite his orders to take you alive, he is past caring about the consequences.

He walks up behind you, with the blade he used to kill his friend, and runs you through.

TONIGHT WAS YOUR LAST ADVENTURE

112

Your opponent drops to the floor, unconscious.

As your opponent hits the ground, you are already moving. You try to force your way through the mob of fighting men, women, orcs, ogres and dwarves.

TEST YOUR AGILITY.
If you pass, you manage to wriggle your way out of the tavern. Write down the Codeword **CON** and turn to **148**
If you fail, turn to **106**

113

You try to sneak out of the church, but then you hear a voice behind you,

"Where are you going, whelp? Leaving so soon?"

You turn and see both the man in blue and the man in brown standing before you.

"*Enoch, this is the one she wants*", says the man in brown "*Yeah, finally*" replies Enoch, *"let's take him*"

They draw their swords in unison.

ENOCH	FIGHTING SKILL	12
	ENDURANCE	14
MAN IN BROWN	FIGHTING SKILL	10
	ENDURANCE	10

If the man in blue gets down to below 4 **ENDURANCE** points, turn to **146**
If you lose, turn to **129**
If you win, turn to **150**

114

You creep around on your belly, slithering like a snake, moving from settle to settle. Soon you are hiding behind the last bench, near to the main door. The man in blue still waits there. You watch, looking under the feet of the pews, and until the man in the brown shirt enters the vestry to check it.

You are now close enough to try a **POTION OF SLEEP**. If you have one, and don't have the Codeword **HEISTER**, and you want to try it, turn to **115**

Otherwise read on,

You think you have at least a few seconds before the man in brown will be able to reach the other end of the church. You silently draw your sword, and jump out at the man in blue.

First you must initially fight the man in blue. He is the toughest opponent you have faced. He snarls at you,

"You think a runt like you can beat one of the Kindness? Let alone two of us? You are a fool, boy. I, Enoch, will send you to meet the Death Goddess early."

But first, roll 2d6 and add 3 to the result, and round the result up. This is how far away the **MAN IN BROWN** is. Each combat round takes 2 seconds. So if you have a score of 14, you can fight just **ENOCH** for 7 rounds, after that the **MAN IN BROWN** will join the fight and you will have to fight them simultaneously.

ENOCH	**FIGHTING SKILL**	12
	ENDURANCE	14
MAN IN BROWN	**FIGHTING SKILL**	10
	ENDURANCE	10

If Enoch gets down to below 4 **ENDURANCE** points, turn to **146**
If you lose, turn to **129**
If you win, turn to **150**

115

You loosen the top of the bottle, and then throw the **POTION OF SLEEP** at the feet of the man in blue. It clinks as it hits the floor, and the top comes off. The acrid smoke fizzes out of the bottle and surrounds the man in blue in a smog.

You cough slightly, as the fog has reached you. Lose 1 **FIGHTING SKILL** until you leave the church.

You stand up, ready to run for the door when the man falls to the floor, but something is wrong. After a few moments the fog dissipates, and the man in blue stands there unaffected. He smiles, coldly,

"Ha, you think a potion can put a fully trained member of the Kindness to sleep? You are a fool, boy. I, Enoch, will send you to the long sleep to meet the Death Goddess"

The man in brown has also returned up the aisle. You must fight both.

ENOCH	**FIGHTING SKILL**	12
	ENDURANCE	14
MAN IN BROWN		
	FIGHTING SKILL	10
	ENDURANCE	10

If Enoch gets down to below 4 **ENDURANCE** points, turn to **146**
If you fail, turn to **129**
If you win, turn to **150**

116

"These are Seth", (the man in black half bows, mockingly), *"and Enoch. I assume you recognize Enoch?"*

The man in blue looks down at you, scowling.

"He certainly remembers you, as you bested him in unarmed combat. He would dearly love a rematch wouldn't you?"

Enoch nods, his eyes never leaving you.

(The man in black just stares down at you with icy eyes), *"They will take you to where you hid this item. They are my most trusted lieutenants, and will have no compunction to slit your throat if you lie. Understand?"*

All reasonableness has fled out of Lilith's voice, which now sounds cold and emotionless.

Turn to **137**

117

The god of luck must be shining on you, as when the Raven withdraws from his most recent attack, then his back leg slips off the ridge. He seems to hang there for an age, but then falls. He makes no sound as he falls to the hard stone, but then he lands with a thud and a groan, two stories down. You peer over the roof, but all you can see is a small pool of blood on the cobbles.

The assassin has disappeared into thin air. A few doors away, you can see a tavern, called the Hanging Gate Inn. You decide to take refuge in it for a while, as the rooftops seem too dangerous.

You stumble into the Hanging Gate, and buy a pint of Evil Eye. This costs you 2 gold pieces. You find a small table out of the way, and nurse your pint.

Turn to **136**

118

You roll straight along the foot wide ridge of the roof, and come up and spin around and drop into a crouch. You draw your sword. A black shadow of a figure stands before you. The assassin jumps at you. This Raven is different, as it has a white headband wrapped around its black hood.

You have to fight.

| **WHITE RAVEN** | **FIGHTING SKILL** | 8 |
| | **ENDURANCE** | 9 |

You are fighting on top of a roof, on a ridgeway that is less than a foot wide. It's very precarious. After each attack round, you must throw 1d6 for you, and 1d6 for your opponent.

If you roll 1, then:
If it's for you, turn to **181**
If it's for the Raven, turn to **117**

Otherwise, carry on fighting. If you win, turn to **126**

119

The book falls flat with a thump, less than two yards from you. The man in blue hears it and reaches for the sword at his waist, and walks down the aisle, keeping his distance from the pews.

You hide yourself as much under the settle as you can, but he's on alert, and he checks behind every bench. He sees you hiding. Grimly, you draw your sword and jump out at him. He quickly ripostes your blade with his. He smiles,

"You think a runt like you can beat one of the Kindness? Let alone two of us? You are a fool, boy. I, Enoch, will send you to meet the Death Goddess early."

First you must initially fight the man in blue. He is the toughest opponent you have faced. He snarls at you,

But first, roll 2d6 and add 3 to the result, and round the result up. This is how far away the **MAN IN BROWN** is. Each combat round takes 2 seconds. So if you have a score of 14, you can fight the Enoch only for 7 rounds, after that the **MAN IN BROWN** will join the fight and you will have to fight them simultaneously.

ENOCH	**FIGHTING SKILL**	12
	ENDURANCE	14
MAN IN BROWN	**FIGHTING SKILL**	10
	ENDURANCE	10

If you lose, turn to **129**
If Enoch gets down to below 4 **ENDURANCE** points, turn to **146**
If you win, turn to **150**

120

TEST YOUR INTELLIGENCE
If you pass, turn to **143**
If you fail, write down the Codeword **FREEBOOTER** and turn to **129**

121

The three Ravens drop down to street level silently. One is in front of you, the other two behind you. They have you trapped in the dark alley. You must fight all of them.

RAVEN 1	FIGHTING SKILL	8
	ENDURANCE	10
RAVEN 2	FIGHTING SKILL	9
	ENDURANCE	13
RAVEN 3	FIGHTING SKILL	10
	ENDURANCE	9

If you are lucky enough to win, turn to **148**
If you fail, write down the Codeword **LOOTER** and turn to **129**

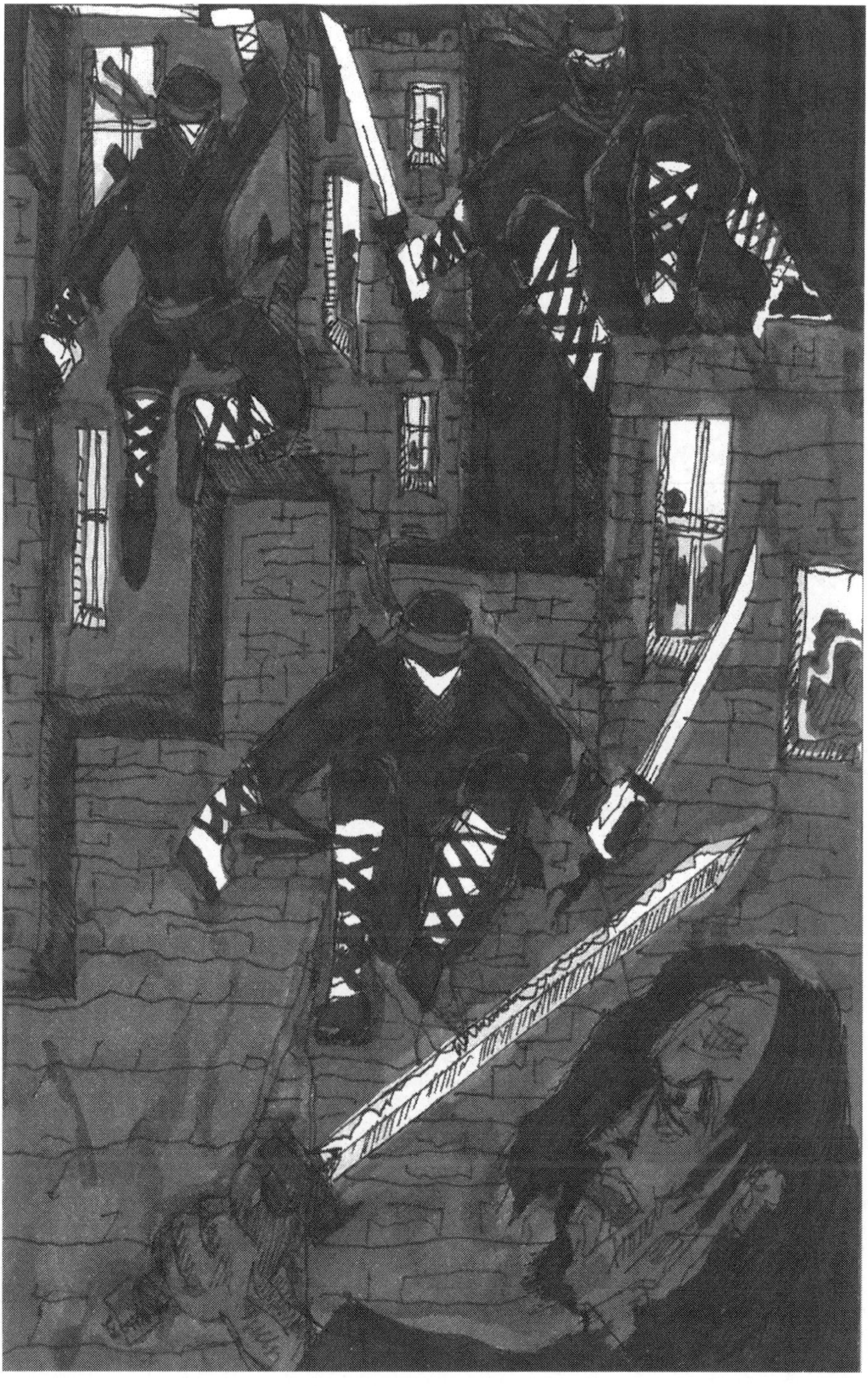

122

It flies exactly as you wanted it to. Staying low, and not hitting the floor for about ten yards. It then skitters down the aisle. It's too quiet for the man in brown to hear, but the man in blue does. He reaches for the sword at his waist, and walks down the aisle. You hide yourself as much under the pew as you can. He comes to a standstill only inches from your outstretched arm. With your razor sharp knife, you slice off a piece of the hem of his cloak.

The man grunts, and returns to the door to resume his vigil.

Quickly, you tie the sliver of material around the neck of the poppet. You peer out and test the effectiveness. The man in blue is standing still, watching the church. The man in brown is still searching the vestry.

You lift the poppets left arm. The man in blues left arm shoots up for the ceiling. He looks confused.

Then you put it down, and lift up the poppet's right leg. Again the man in blue does the same, shock registering on his face.

Then you alternate the two. You cannot help but laugh silently, as he does a little jig on the spot, confusion on his face. He tries to cry out, but the mouth of the poppet is sewn shut, and so he cannot even raise a murmur.

You stand up from behind the pew, and his eyes widen in surprise, fear and rage. You wave at him. He doesn't move and so you lift his right hand up and force him to wave back at you. The man in blue's eyes narrow in fury. You really shouldn't tempt tease him, but you need time to learn how to control your new toy.

Then you hear a cry from behind. The man in brown has appeared from the vestry and seen you. He draws his sword, and sprints up the aisle. You hop over the last pew, and get behind the man in blue. You make him draw his sword, which is a bit tricky initially.

The man in brown shouts,

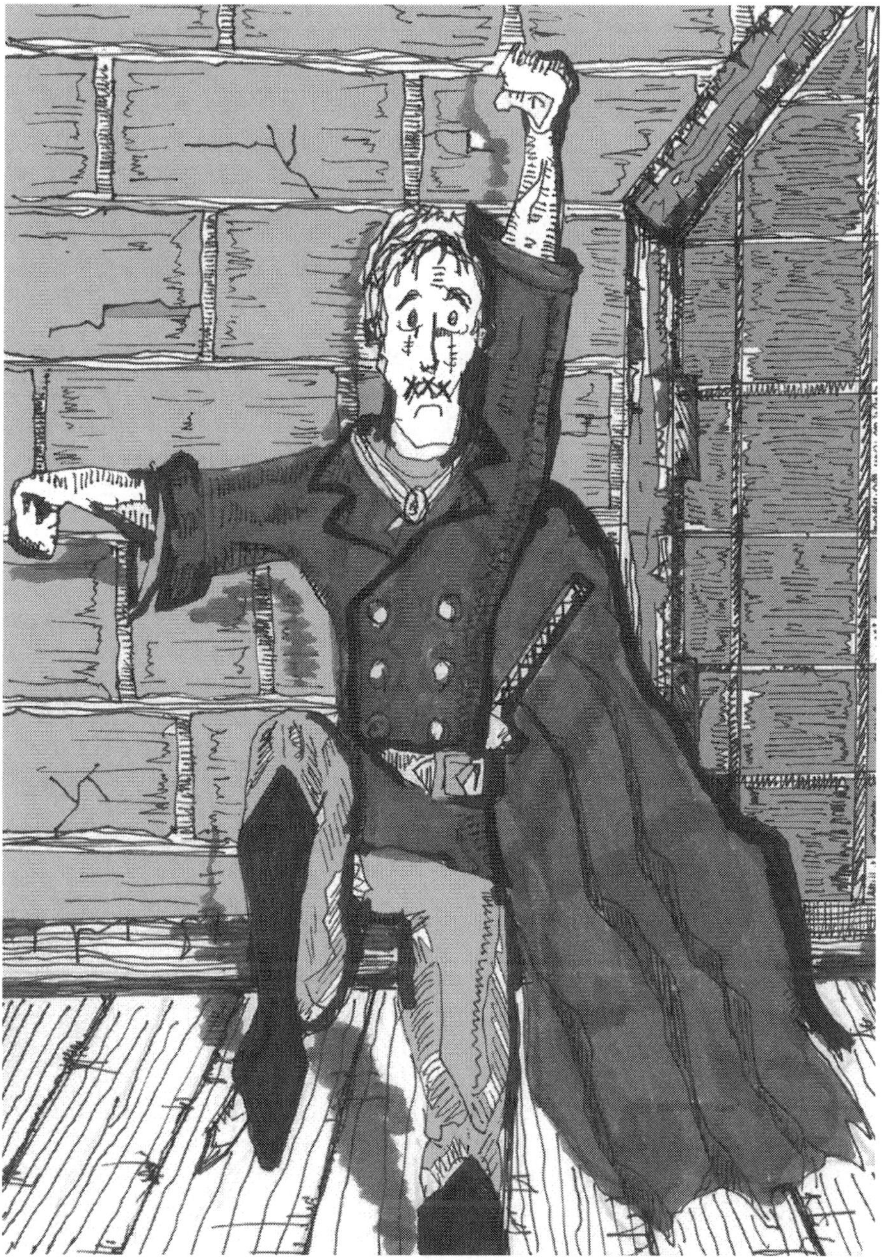

"What are you doing, Enoch? Why are you protecting that street rat? You know we have our orders to bring him to her."

Enoch can only moan.

You must use the man in blue to try to defeat the man in brown. However whilst you have control over the man's body, you don't have his skill, and so you must fight with your own.

You stand behind Enoch, and raise his sword arm. Enoch complies, albeit a bit jerkily the first time. However, you soon get the hang of it. It's almost fun, fighting with little risk. The man in brown obviously finds it a bit eerie and scary, as he doesn't seem to attack with the fluidity and skill you would expect. He seems a nervous wreck.

If Enoch is killed by the Man in Brown, then you will have to fight him yourself.

ENOCH	**FIGHTING SKILL**	Shadows
	ENDURANCE	14
MAN IN BROWN	**FIGHTING SKILL**	6
	ENDURANCE	8

If you win, write down the Codeword **CARDSHARP**, and turn to **105**
If you lose, turn to **129**

123

If you have the Codeword **DIPPER**, turn to **17** now

If not, read on,

Two figures stand before you. You recognize them as bruisers who frequent the taverns by the dockside. They are known as bashers and brawlers for hire. Silently, they close in on you, wielding foot long cudgels.

You draw your blade, but you feel a bit dizzy. There must have been something in your drink. Lose 2 **FIGHTING SKILL** for this fight.

RUFFIAN 1	**FIGHTING SKILL**	7
	ENDURANCE	7
RUFFIAN 2	**FIGHTING SKILL**	8
	ENDURANCE	8

If you have the Codeword **FENCE**, after 2 rounds of fighting, turn to **61**
If you have the Codeword **CORSAIR,** after the first round of fighting, turn to **68**
Note down this reference.

If you lose, you are dead
If you win, turn to **66**

124

The hairs on the back of your neck prick up all of a sudden. You react without thinking. You drop and roll forward. Just in time, as a sword hisses above you.

TEST YOUR AGILITY. If you have the **SKILL OF SPEED AND AGILITY**, you can reduce the roll by one
If you pass, turn to **118**
If you fail, write down the Codeword **CHEAT** and turn to **129**

125

You watch carefully and then when all of Seth's weight is on the suspect rung, you kick downwards.

TEST YOUR FORTUNE. If you pass, turn to **152**
If you fail, turn to **153**

126

You quickly search the Ravens body. You pull back the mask, and find the face of a boy, no more than 14 years old. You feel regret having killed someone so young. You assume that the white headband must mean a novice assassin. Their forces must be spread thin to find you, if they are using inexperienced guild members.

The Ravens are obviously looking for you in this direction. You can either go back and take the other way, or climb down from the roof and take refuge in a tavern.

If you want to go back the other way on the roof, turn to **130**
If you want to jump down into the street, turn to **109**

127

The jump is only a matter of 8 or so yards, and so you clear it easily. However your pursuers are closing on you. Then all of a sudden, you feel something pull your leg. A hook has caught the top of your soft boots. The Raven pulls the silken cord attached to the hook, and you stumble forward.

You fall heavily on the roof, and then bounce off a porch halfway down before landing with a thud in the dark alley below. Lose 2 **ENDURANCE** points.

Turn to **121**

128

Two men walk forward. You recognize them as the man in blue and the man in black who started the brawl at the tavern.

If you have the Codeword **DESPOILER**, turn to **116**
If not, read on,

"These are Seth" (the man in black half bows, mockingly), *"and Enoch"* (the man in blue just stares down at you with icy eyes), *"you may recognize them. They will take you to where you hid this item. They are my most trusted lieutenants, and will have no compunction to slit your throat if you lie. Understand?"*

All reasonableness has fled out of Lilith's voice, which now sounds cold and emotionless.

Turn to **137**

129

Turn to the correct reference depending on which Codeword you have:

If you have the Codeword **CHEAT**, turn to **183**
If you have the Codeword **LOOTER**, turn to **184**
If you have the Codeword **LARCENER**, turn to **185**
If you have the Codeword **FREEBOOTER**, turn to **2**
If you don't have the any of these Codewords, turn to **187**

130

You head right along the rooftops. You turn and think you can see dark shadows following across the rooftops. For once, you don't feel safe up here.

You come to a jump across a street to a lower level. Do you want to:
Jump it, turn to **127**
Drop down to street level, turn to **139**

131

A couple of hours after you leave the One Eyed Rat, you are trying to sleep in a safe-house not far away. But something is keeping your mind restless.

You sit up and get out of the pallet that serves as a make-shift bed. You walk over to the table. On it is the journal you stole from Malombr's office last night.

You flick through its thick vellum pages, noting it just seems to be a sales ledger. It's written in an elegant hand, in dark ink, and just gives names, produce and cost. There's nothing of interest of or use, unless someone would be interested in a shipment of oats or beans. You had hoped it would document something of more interest. You sigh and go to close the book.

TEST YOUR INTELLIGENCE. If you have the **SKILL OF DIVVY**, you can reduce the roll by 2.

If you pass, turn to **198**
If you fail, turn to **173**

132

You recognize two of the three men from the Hanging Gate. You swear to yourself. It's obviously no longer coincidence, they must be hunting you. Only the best Ravens are reputed to work in plain sight. You must be cautious.

At least you are forewarned that they are dangerous.
Write down the Codeword **HEISTER**.

Turn to **140**

133

But then you stop for a moment and reconsider. You know these two are Ravens, and likely to be two of the best of their Guild. You will need every advantage.

If you have the Codeword **CHISLER**, turn to **135**
Otherwise, turn to **114**

134

You lean against the wall, panting with the effort. Somehow you are still alive. You take the small, silk wrapped item out of your pocket, and think about opening it. You decide otherwise.

Turn to **168**

135

Silently, you rummage around in your bag and find the small doll. You recognize it as a poppet, a small figure that can be used to control others. However you need some part or belonging of the other person to control them.

You creep around on your belly, slithering like a snake, moving from settle to settle. Soon you are hiding behind the last bench, near to the main door. The man in blue still waits there. You watch, looking under the feet of the pews, until the man in the brown shirt enters the vestry to check it.

You see a small prayer book on the floor and pick it up. You flatly throw it down the side isle, away from the main door.

TEST YOUR INTELLIGENCE
If you pass, turn to **122**
If you fail, turn to **119**

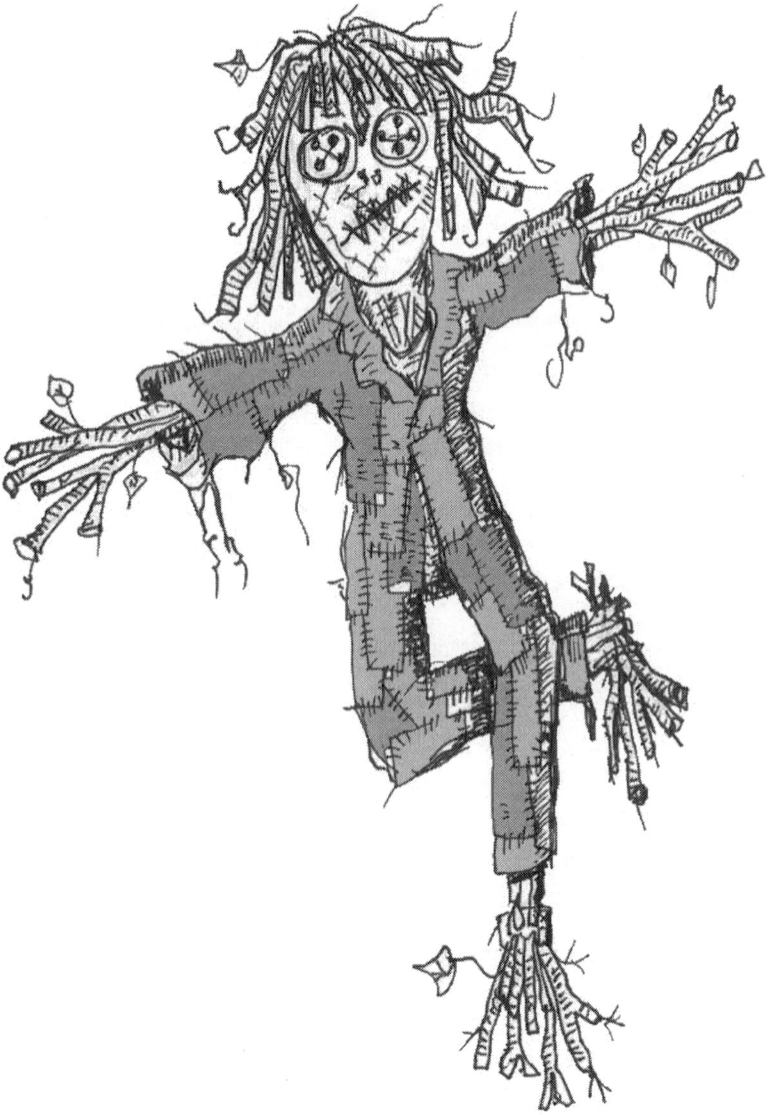

136

As you sit there, nursing your beer and watching the room, you notice three men enter. They seem to enter as a group, but as soon as they are in the taproom, they all split up. All are regular looking men, average height, non-descript brown hair, unremarkable faces. However, as they split up they all seem to be searching the room.

The one in a black jerkin heads to the right of the room. Another, in brown, to the left. The final one, in blue, walks down the centre of the room towards the bar. He orders, and turns to lean with his back against the bar, holding his beer – which he does not even sip. His eyes roam the room, and then they stop on you. You feel a recognition flash between you.

Then the man in blue turns to the man next to him at the bar.

"What did you say, you scum?" he shouts at the man, who turns confused. The man in blue smashes his tankard straight into the poor man's face. He staggers back, his lips bleeding. Seemingly at a signal, the man in blue's companions also start fights in their parts of the room. Soon, the whole of the taproom is in chaos.

Bar fights are common in Laeveni, especially in the lower city. However, there are rules, of an informal sort. No one dares draw a weapon, as if anyone is stabbed, or brained, then the Watch will soon arrive. You are allowed to use your fists, and anything lying around such as a tankard, chair or table. It's also an unwritten rule that if someone drops unconscious, then they are left alone.

The fight soon reaches your table, and you stand up ready to defend yourself. You see both the man in blue and his friend in brown are heading across the room towards you.

Roll 1d6, and turn to **196**

137

They untie you, Enoch is not particularly gentle as he loosens the knots in the ropes. All the time, his eyes never leave you.

You stand up, and the ropes fall away from you. You flex your muscles, to restore the circulation to your limbs, and limber up. You have been stripped of all your weapons, and they have been thorough. Then you stagger forward and almost fall. They nearly killed you when they took you, and your injuries are badly effecting you.

Lilith looks at Enoch, and nods once. He scowls, but produces a black leather flask studded in silver. He uncaps it, and grabs your jaw forcing it open. He pours a burning liquid down your throat. You nearly pass out with the pain, but then you start to recover. Your wounds start to close up, scab over and then heal, all in a matter of moments. You feel as though you did at the start of the night. In perfect health.

You can restore your **ENDURANCE** back to its full level.

"You are indeed a fortunate man. Few outside of our Guild ever taste that. However, you may find it has unexpected effects." smiles Lilith.

Write down the Codeword **MEDDLER**.

As good as you feel, you reason that you will not be able to outfight them, or probably outpace then in a race, but you may be able to outthink them.

They lead you out of the room, from the normal street house. Soon you are on the roads, and you lead the way.

You are soon at the bakery. You normally enter via the street, but there is also an outside ladder up to the roof. You get to the ladder, and point up. Seth and Enoch converse briefly between themselves.

"I will lead", says Enoch coldly, **"then you, my friend, and Seth will be behind you. Any funny stuff, and you will regret it lad."**

You agree. Enoch starts up the ladder. The ladder is old and wooden and in poor repair. Soon you are at the third floor. The attic is on the fourth. Enoch has nearly reached the roof, and Seth is still close behind you. As you put your foot on the next rung, you feel it give a little, as the wood starts to break.

You hide the fact that it's weak, and carry on. Enoch is on the roof, looking around for the hatch. Seth is about to put his foot onto the weakened rung.

Do you want to?
Kick down at him, hoping that the increased weight will break the rung. Turn to **125**
Drop down, putting all your weight on Seth, and hoping you can hold on if the rung breaks. Turn to **151**
Carry on climbing the ladder, turn to **197**

138

You wake up, not knowing how long you have been unconscious, but all of a sudden you are roused in the most old fashioned of ways. The cold bucket of water wakes you up as the contents are tipped on your head. You have a headache, and feel a bit beaten up, but apart from that, no serious injuries

Your **ENDURANCE** score returns to the level it was before the fight in the tavern.

Two voices laugh, and you recognized them

"Now told you Erv! Bucket of water never fails", laughs Carv.
"We saw you woz in trouble young fella, and as we owed you a pint back, we managed to grab you and pull you out." grunts Erv
"Good fight, though", continues Carv
"Aye, best for some time. Shall we go back in?"
"Why not? Before the Watch gets here"
"See you later, fella. Next time, maybe pick on someone smaller to fight", laughs Erv

And the two burly soldiers wave at you, and turn and run back into the tavern, with Carv shouting *"C'mon you ugly bunch, who's next?"*

Write down the Codeword **CON**

Turn to **148**

139

Instead of taking the jump, you slip down to street level, as you are out of sight of your pursuers for a few moments. You head towards a dark alley.

TEST YOUR AGILITY. If you have the **SKILL of HIDING IN SHADOWS**, you can remove 2 from the roll.

If you pass, turn to **110**
If you fail, turn to **121**

140

The figure in blue stays at the door, and directs the man in brown to search the church. It's only a small church for the commoners, with just one floor and no balcony. The altar is slightly raised at the far end, and there's one single door, presumably to the vestry.

Your options are:
Fight, turn to **193**
Try to sneak out of the front door, turn to **113**

141

You reach out and pull the left lever. A panel opens. You reach in and grab two things. The silk wrapped object, and a long object wrapped in leather. Then you quickly pull the right lever. The floor panel beneath you drops away to form an angled slide. You slip down the escape hole, and slide down the chute. You pick up speed as you travel down, and soon you are spat out through a flap in the wall, into a back alley.

Lose 2 **ENDURANCE**.

You are soon on your feet, aware that Enoch and Seth will be following you down the chute. You have moments. You untie the leather package, and inside is a gleaming sword, sheathed. It is one your great friend and fellow adventurer, Vostede Mesmo, gave you at the end of last year's adventures. You treasure it more than any other item, and so never use it. But now, you pull the sword from the sheath and stand ready.

While using this sword, you will gain an increase of 2 **FIGHTING SKILL**. It is an exceptional blade.

You leap back up, sure that Enoch will follow down the chute. Sure enough, Enoch soon drops through the panel, into the alley. He grunts as he hits the ground heavily, but rolls with grace and comes to his feet, sword already drawn.

If you have the Codeword **SOOT**, turn to **188**
If not, turn to **189**

142

Left takes you into the merchant's quarters, back to where you were earlier tonight. It may be a bit of a risk if the scene at Malombr's house has been discovered. Still, you hope that the Ravens will not think you will revisit near the scene.

The night is still and quiet, and the moon is half, shedding a bit of light on the rooftops. You can see ahead of you that you seem to be alone on the thieve's road, above the city. You hurry along the ridges of the roofs, passing lightly as you go.

If you have the **SKILL OF SIXTH SENSE**, turn to **124**
If not, turn to **164**

143

It is just as well that you took the time to attach a wire to the door. As soon as it's pulled opened, the wire tenses and pulls over a candlestick near the door. It crashes to the ground.

However, if your **ENDURANCE** is 8 or less, write down the Codeword **FREEBOOTER** and turn to **129**

Otherwise read on,

You awaken immediately, and slip off the settle, and hide in the shadows. The door continues to open, and two figures walk inside.

If you have the Codeword **CON**, turn to **132**
If not, read on

They are both regular looking men, average height, non-descript brown hair, unremarkable faces. However, as they split up they all seem to be searching the room. One is wearing a blue jerkin, and the other, a brown jacket.

Turn to **140**

144

You draw your sword and stand out in plain view of them men.

"Well, look here, Enoch, this is the one she wants", says the man in brown
"**Yeah, finally**" replies Enoch, **"let's take him."**

They draw their swords in unison.

ENOCH	FIGHTING SKILL	12
	ENDURANCE	14
MAN IN BROWN	FIGHTING SKILL	10
	ENDURANCE	10

If the man in blue gets down to below 4 **ENDURANCE** points, turn to **146**
If you lose, turn to **129**
If you win, turn to **150**

145

You draw your sword. Lilith laughs.

"You seek to fight me? Really Shadow, I expected more of you. But if this is the way you choose, then so be it."

She draws two swords from her belt.

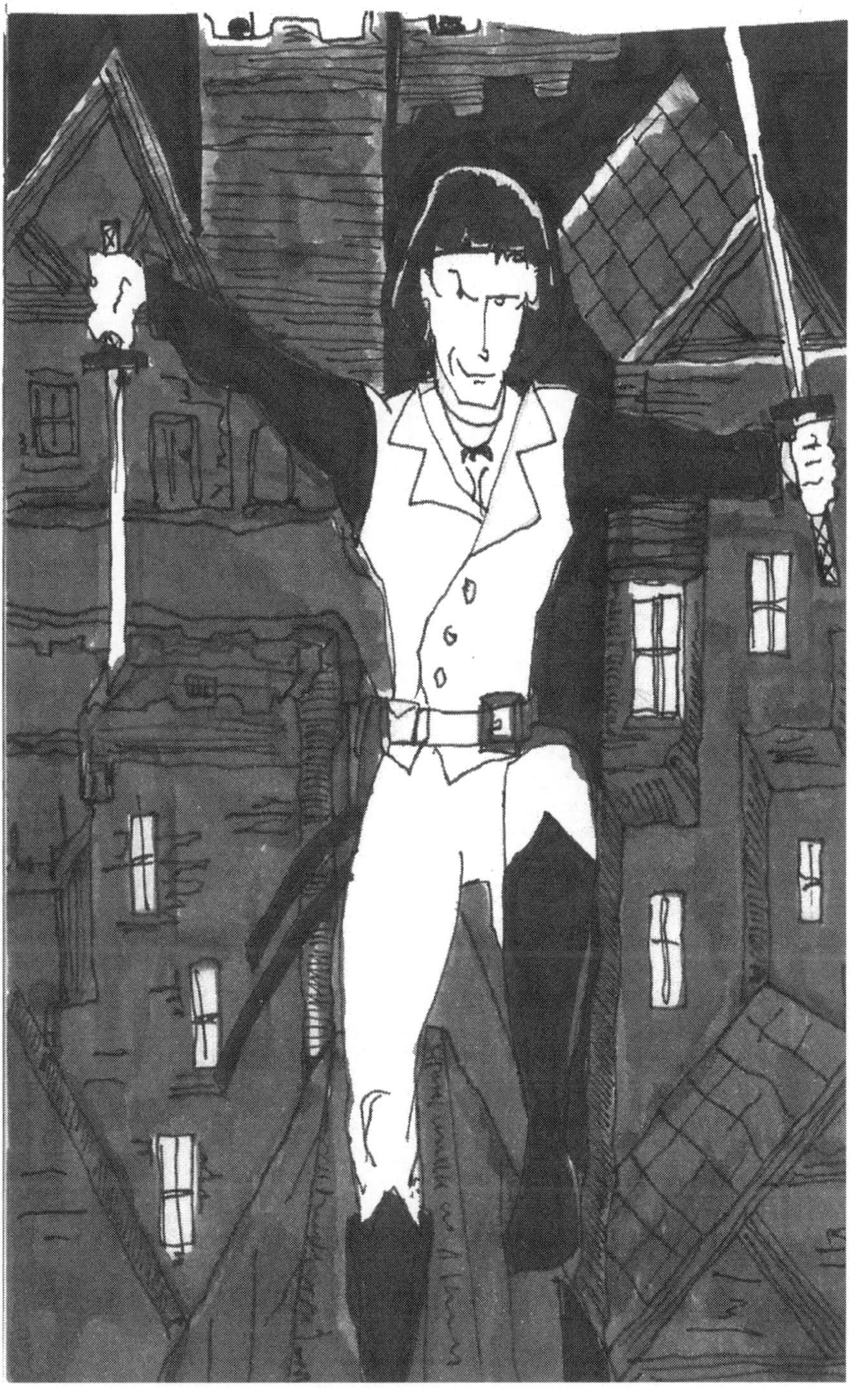

"You will find I am a lot harder to beat than my servants"

LILITH   **FIGHTING SKILL**   **17**
                ENDURANCE   **25**

If you win, turn to **170**
If you lose,
TONIGHT IS YOUR LAST ADVENTURE

146

All of a sudden, the man in blue disengages from the fight and runs for the door. He pushes it open, and sprints out onto the street.

If you are still fighting the man in brown, turn to **113**, and finish the fight.

If the man in brown is already dead, turn to **150**

147

"A ruddy marine" spluttered one of soldiers, (Erv you think, although your head is still a bit woozy)
"And you were caught with his wife! HA! Good on you lad. Those salt eaters are nothing but popinjays in their fancy naval uniforms. We soldiers do all the proper fighting", continues Carv (again, you think)
"As it ever was," agrees Erv, but then continues, *"even so, maybe we should take-"*

"My good fellows, for your help, maybe I could buy you a drink in that tavern", you quickly say, feeling that the moment is getting away from you.

"One wouldn't harm, Erv"
"Suppose not, Carv"

You stumble into the Hanging Gate, and buy them each a pint of Evil Eye bitter.

This, plus your drink, costs you 6 gold pieces. They thank you, but then see some friends on the other side of the taproom. Erv claps you on the shoulder, which makes you wince, and Carv shakes your hand, and they take their leave. You find a small table out of the way, and nurse your pint.

Write down the Codeword **BRIGAND**

Turn to **136**

148

You turn the other way, and walk along the street, trying to look inconspicuous. You decide to take refuge for a while.

Taking stock of where you are, you see a church opposite. By church rules, the doors of any place of worship must be open in case worshippers want to pray. Given the time, you suspect the church will be almost deserted.

Feeling every ache and pain on your body, you creep over to the church, and pull open the large wooden door, and slip inside.

The inside of the church is dark and cool, lit by only a few candles. It's only a small church, known as the Chapel of Devero, and not very grand. However you take the chance to rest.

If you have any food, you can eat to try to recover some **ENDURANCE**. You can only eat one portion of food.

If you have the **SKILL OF CHAKRA**, then you have time to try to heal some of your wounds. However, there is a price for this. For every 2 points of **ENDURANCE** you recover, you lose 1 point from another attribute.

Roll 1d6 to see how many **ENDURANCE** Points you recover.

Now roll to see which other **ABILITY**, if any, has been effected.

ROLL	ABILITY
1	FIGHTING SKILL
2	AGILITY
3	FITNESS
4	INTELLIGENCE
5	FORTUNE
6	NO EFFECT

You lay down on one of the settles, and soon you nod off into a doze.
An hour or so later, the door handle twists and someone starts to pull the door open. It's hinges creaks slightly.

You are still fast asleep.

Turn to **120**

149

You fall, and twist and twist and turn, but you hit the hard stone street hard. Roll 1d6 and reduce your **ENDURANCE** by this number.

You try to stand up, but find strong arms grab you and haul you to your feet. Two off duty soldiers hold you up. You glance up, and see the assassin's head disappear over the roof edge, and see the shadowy form run off over the roof tops. This was obviously too public for him, as you have landed in a busy street.

"Now now, what's this, Erv?" says the first.
"Not so sure Carv, it seems to be raining street rats tonight", laughs the second.
"What do you reckon we should do with him?"
"Well, rightfully, we should take him in, but having just come off duty-"

You start to come to your senses.
"Good gentlemen, thank you for your help. I had to make a rather quick exit from my lady friend's window, and seem to have slipped and fallen."
They look at you suspiciously, but also half curious.
You continue,
"Sadly, my friend's husband returned earlier than expected. He is a marine in the navy, and got to shore sooner than she expected"

You hope you can gain their sympathy, as land soldiers traditionally hate marines, and that hatred is reciprocated.

If you have the **SKILL of CHARM AND GUILE**, turn to **147**
If not, turn to **107**

150

You lean against the wall, panting with the effort. Then you leave the church. You head straight to the safe-house where you stored the mysterious object earlier this night. You run across the rooftops and drop into the attic of the local bakery run by Leff Rawls. You recover the item from a hidey hole. You think about opening it. You decide otherwise. You put it inside your jacket.

Turn to **168**

151

When Seth has his foot on the unsafe rung, you drop down with all your weight. You land heavily on Seth's head, and he grunts. You hear a crack, as the rung gives under the increased weight.

TEST YOUR AGILITY. If you have the **SKILL OF SPEED AND AGILITY**, then you can take 1 off the roll.
If you pass, turn to **163**
If you fail, turn to **38**

152

You time your kick just right. It catches Seth on the top of the head, just as he has all his weight on one foot. The additional force makes the rung start to splinter. But it's not enough.
You try again.

This time it works. The rung breaks, and Seth foot drops down. The sudden change of weight means that Seth loses his grip on the ladder. He starts to topple backwards.

TEST YOUR FORTUNE again.
If you pass, turn to **67**
If you fail, turn to **38**

153

Seth begins to fall, but as he does, he manages to grab hold of your foot. You frantically try to grasp the ladder, but his weight is too much.

You both fall, and smash onto the hard cobbled stones below.

Enoch above hears the noise, and looks out of the attic. He sees you and Seth entangled on the floor, unmoving. Carefully he makes his way down the broken ladder, reaches inside your tunic. He finds the silk package, and walks off without a further look back.

Lilith will be pleased with him. He almost smiles.

TONIGHT WAS YOUR LAST ADVENTURE

154

You decide to head down the stairs. You take them carefully, and they curve around until they reach a landing half way down. Straight in front of you is an half-orc guard. He is staggering around, with foam bubbling from his mouth. His eyes look confused, but then he sees you and snarls. He draws his serrated bastard sword, and lunges at you.

As he does, you notice a small black barb in the half-orcs neck. A poison dart!

However then he's on you and you must fight him. Luckily he's confused and weakened, otherwise this would have been a sterner test. Grimly you draw your sword, which looks like a short dagger compared to your opponents.

HALF-ORC BODY GUARD	**FIGHTING SKILL**	**7**
	ENDURANCE	**8**

If you have the Codeword **CORSAIR,** after the first round of fighting, turn to **68**
If you have the Codeword **FENCE**, after 2 rounds of fighting, turn to **61**
Note down this reference.
If you win, turn to **18**

155

If you have the Codeword **DIPPER**, turn to **17** straight away.
If not, read on,

You land lightly in the alley and you decide it would be best to get off the streets for now. You think about either taking the rooftops or the sewers. But before you can move, a dark shadow falls over you. You look around and see two heavy set men. They close on you, armed with cudgels, and you start to draw you sword.

You recognize them as local strong-arms from the harbour area, often used to press-gang people. You dislike press-gangers.

You must fight them.

RUFFIAN 1	**FIGHTING SKILL**	**7**
	ENDURANCE	**7**
RUFFIAN 2	**FIGHTING SKILL**	**8**
	ENDURANCE	**8**

If you have the Codeword **FENCE**, after 2 rounds of fighting, turn to **61**
If you have the Codeword **CORSAIR,** after the first round of fighting, turn to **68**
Note down this reference.

If you win, turn to **66**

156

Deciding you need to rest, you head towards the nearby Jackdaws safe-house. They are dotted around the city, normally in the sewers, and used to store equipment, stores and herbs, as well as to stash loot.

Its only 150 yards, although it's hard to tell in the dark. You get there. The bolt hole is hidden by an old half rotting pallet, which is in fact far more sturdy on closer inspection. You find the hidden lock, and there's a click as the disguised door swings open. You slip inside.

You light the lamp inside, carefully ventilated from the gas in the sewer, and take time to recover.

If you are wounded, you find some herbs and bathe your wounds, allowing you to recover 4 **ENDURANCE**.

You also find a stash of gold, and put 20 gold pieces in your purse, just in case.

You rest until you haven't heard a noise outside for some time, and feel a lot improved.
You open the door of the bolt hole and head out.

If you have the **SKILL OF FORBEARANCE**, you have waited long enough for any other assassin to leave. You make your way back up to street level. Write down the Codeword **CROCODILE**, and turn to **66**

Otherwise, **TEST YOUR AGILITY**
If you pass, turn to **177**
If you fail, turn to **95**

157

Taking your time, you inch across the floor until you are within striking range. You raise your sword and prepare to bring it down. However just as you do, Malombr sees you and his eye's widen. The Raven is alert to this and turns and crouches down. His sword whistles out of his back sheath with almost preternatural speed.

TEST YOUR FIGHTING SKILL. If you pass, then you manage to bring down your sword and injure the Raven. You can subtract 1 from his **FIGHTING SKILL** and 3 from his **ENDURANCE** below.

"You dare to cross a member of the Kindness when he is on his holy work?" hisses the assassin, *"then you shall also meet the death goddess soon."*

He launches himself at you. He is a formidable opponent and it will take some skill and no small fortune to beat him

RAVEN	FIGHTING SKILL	10
	ENDURANCE	12

If you have the Codeword **CORSAIR,** after the first round of fighting, turn to **68**
If you have the Codeword **FENCE**, after 2 rounds of fighting, turn to **61**
Note down this reference.

If you win, turn to **35**

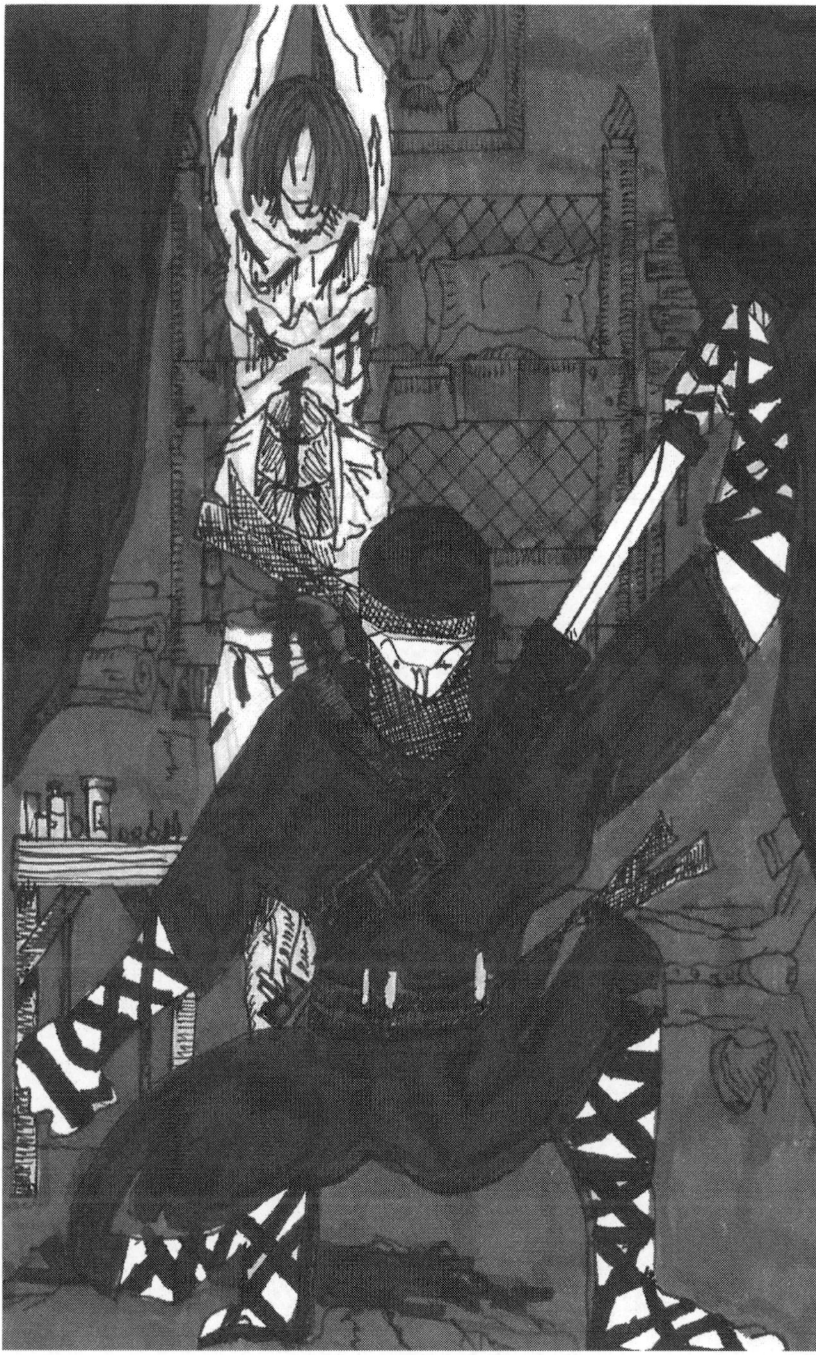

158

This time it works. The rung breaks, and Seth's foot drops down. The sudden change of weight means that Seth loses his grip on the ladder. He falls backwards. Falling to his death. He lands with a thud, some distance below.

Enoch hears the scream of his friend, and looks down from the rooftop. You climb up, safely.

"What happened? What did you do to Seth?"

"Me, nothing." You reply earnestly. *"It looks like the ladder gave way. Look, the rung down there is broken. I nearly fell myself."*

Enoch scowls at you, seemingly his favorite expression.

If you have the **SKILL OF CHARM AND GUILE**, turn to **104**
If not, **TEST ENOCH'S INTELLIGENCE.** He has an **INTELLIGENCE** of 8.
If he passes, then turn to **104**
If he fails, turn to **86**

159

You dodge out of the way, but the flour bag catches Enoch with a glancing blow. He is knocked backwards. Whilst he is on the floor, you turn to the brick wall, and push in a brick. Another panel opens, and inside is a spare sword. At least you can fight him armed.

Enoch rolls with grace and comes to his feet, sword already drawn.

"Now we will have a reckoning, runt", he smiles, without humour.

ENOCH	**FIGHTING SKILL**	**12**
	ENDURANCE	**10**

If you have either of the Codewords **CARDSHARP** or **DESPOILER**, then Enoch gains 1 **FIGHTING SKILL** due to his thirst for revenge.
If you have both, he gains 2 **FIGHTING SKILL**

If you win, turn to **169**
If you lose, turn to **166**

160

You reach out and pull the left lever, a panel opens. You reach in and grab the silk wrapped object, leaving everything else, but then you quickly pull the right lever. The floor panel beneath you drops away to form an angled slide. You slip down the escape hole, and slide down the chute. You pick up speed as you travel down, and soon you are spat out through a flap in the wall, into a back alley.

Lose 2 **ENDURANCE**.

You leap back up, sure that Enoch will follow down the chute. Seth's body is nearby, too fresh even for the scavengers of the city to pick over. His sword is still at his belt, and so you grab the hilt and draw it. At least you can fight Enoch armed.

Sure enough, Enoch soon drops through the panel, into the alley. He grunts as he hits the ground heavily, but rolls with grace and comes to his feet, sword already drawn.

"Now we will have a reckoning, runt", he smiles, without humour.

ENOCH	**FIGHTING SKILL**	12
	ENDURANCE	12

If you have either of the Codewords **CARDSHARP** or **DESPOILER**, then Enoch gains 1 **FIGHTING SKILL** due to his thirst for revenge. If you have both, he gains 2 **FIGHTING SKILL**

If you win, turn to **134**
If you lose, turn to **166**

161

You reach out and pull the right lever. A large bag of flour drops from the ceiling, where it has been hanging by a rope.

TEST YOUR AGILITY. If you pass, turn to **159**
If you fail, turn to **167**

162

You reach out and pull both levers. A large bag of flour drops from the ceiling, where it had been hanging by a rope. Its 100 pound weight flattens both you and Enoch, as he was standing right behind you, as he didn't trust you.

TONIGHT WAS YOUR LAST ADVENTURE

163

If you don't have the **SKILL OF RESILIENCE**, and also have the Codeword **CAT**, turn to **102** now.

Otherwise read on
You grab hold of the side of the ladder with your left hand. Pain shoots through your arm as your shoulder is very nearly dislocated. Lose 2 **ENDURANCE** points.

You hear Seth land with a thud, some distance below.

Enoch hears the scream of his friend, and looks down from the rooftop. You recover, and climb up, safely, nursing your arm.

"What happened? What did you do to Seth?"

"Me, nothing." You reply earnestly. *"It looks like the ladder gave way. Look, the rung down there is broken. I nearly fell myself."*

Enoch scowls at you, seemingly his favorite expression.

Turn to **156**

164

As you run across the roof, you are too busy trying to work out the puzzle has been tonight. It's the last thing that goes through your mind, as a razor sharp short sword cuts through your neck.

The Raven walks from behind the chimney he was concealed behind. She will not be happy. Orders were to capture the little thief, but he was surprisingly fast and the killing stroke was the only option.

The Raven turns, preparing himself as this may be his night to go to the Dark Mistress, along with the thief. But he will not be welcomed into the realm of death as he has failed. Such are the prices for consorting with dark powers.

TONIGHT WAS YOUR LAST ADVENTURE

165

You manage to grab onto the sign. It wrenches your shoulder. Lose 2 **ENDURANCE**.

The Raven walks to the edge of the roof, and sees you hanging there. He grunts, seeing no option. He cannot reach you and in moments you will fall into the street – and the street is busy with revelers. If the little thief is caught, then this would be bad for his Lady.

But you know nothing of this as you hang there, grip slipping. The Raven leans forward, and sticks you through the neck with his sword. You drop to the ground with a thud. The Raven melts back from the roof edge before passersby look up. There are several gasps from below, as your body lands.

She will not be happy. Orders were to capture the little thief, but he was out of reach and the killing stroke was the only option.

The Raven turns, preparing himself as this may be his night to go to the Dark Mistress, along with the thief. But he will not be welcomed into the realm of death as he has failed. Such are the prices for consorting with the dark powers.

TONIGHT WAS YOUR LAST ADVENTURE

166

Enoch grabs you by the throat, and drags you to the hatch into the loft.

"You cursed rat," he screams at you on the floor, as the life ebbs out of you, *"Seth was my friend. We made our first kill together when we were 12. We trained together. Lived together. Loved together. Your last moments will hurt."*

They do indeed. He slowly tortures your almost dead body, until death is finally a release.

Enoch grunts with satisfaction. But then he calms down and realises his error. Lilith will not be pleased with him unless he finds the item. He grimaces.

It must be here somewhere. He searches the attic for hours and eventually finds a secret panel. Behind it are two levers. He almost smiles. He pulls one of them. A great bag of flour drops from the roof, and crushes him.

Tonight it seems, no one wins.

TONIGHT WAS YOUR LAST ADVENTURE

167

A large bag of flour drops from the ceiling, where it had been hanging by a rope. Its 100 pound weight flattens you.

TONIGHT WAS YOUR LAST ADVENTURE

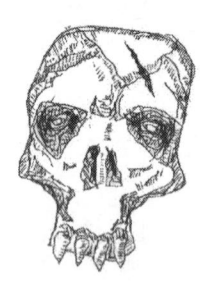

168

Its nearly dawn, and you haven't seen any further Ravens for some hours. You think you may have outsmarted them, and you may be safe. You sit on the roof by the harbour, overlooking the One Eyed Rat, and consider going down and having a pint.

It's been an eventful night, but you still have made some profit. You finger the small parcel in your pocket, still wondering what to do with it.

"**Hello, Shadow**", says a voice.

Turn to **174**

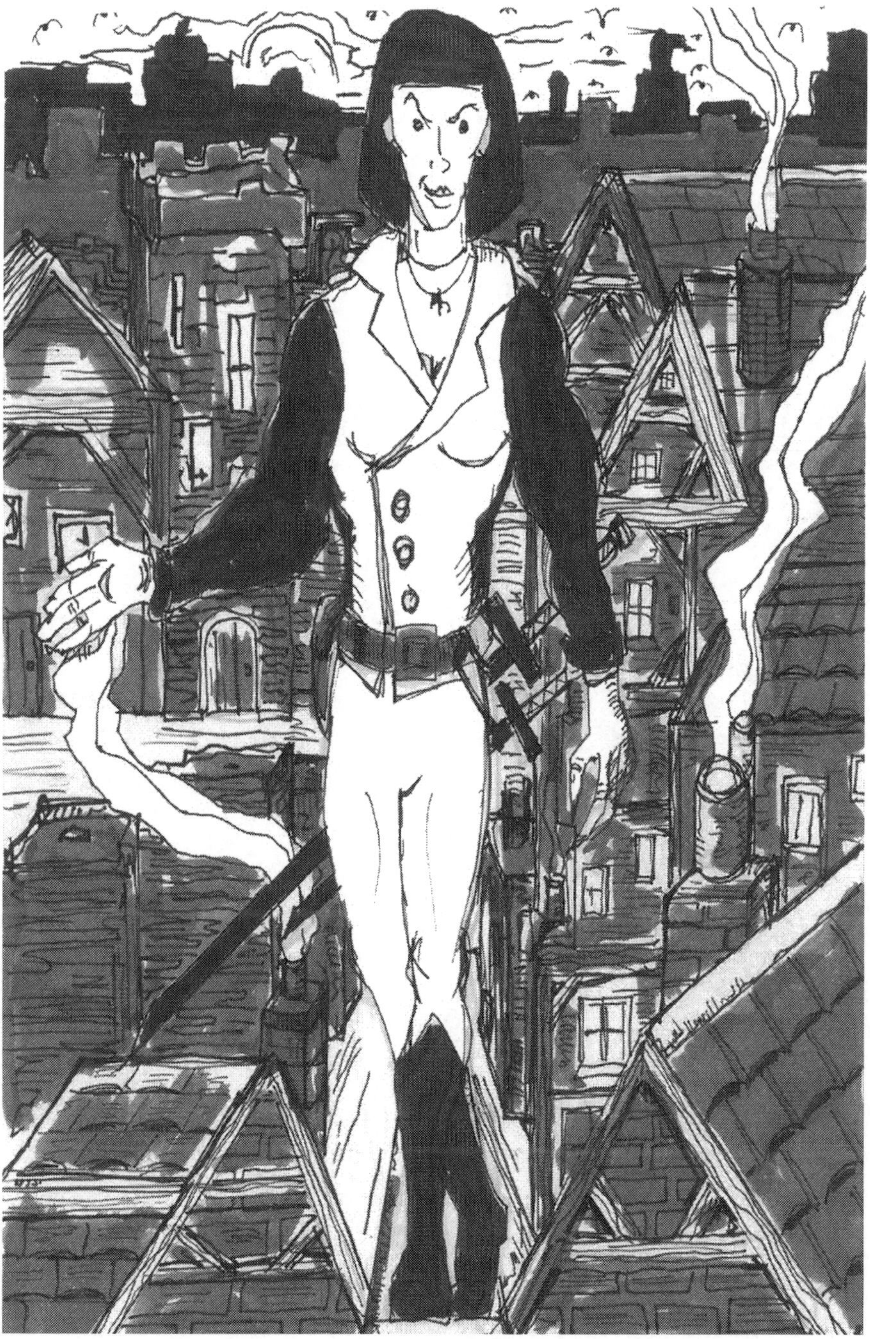

169

You lean against the wall, panting with the effort. He was a terrible opponent, but somehow you have bested him. You pull the correct lever for the hidden panel, and it opens. You take the small, silk wrapped item out of the cubby hole, and think about opening it. You decide otherwise, and put it in your pocket.

Turn to **168**

170

I don't believe you. Try again and don't cheat!
If you didn't cheat, I am really impressed.

Turn to **100**

171

Taking your time, you inch across the floor until you are nearly within striking range. But before you are close enough, Malombr sees you and his eyes widen. The Raven is alert to this and turns and crouches down, and his sword whistles out of his back sheath with almost preternatural speed.

"You dare to cross a member of the Kindness when he is on his holy work?" hisses the assassin, *"Then you shall also meet the death goddess soon."*

He launches himself at you. He is a formidable opponent and it will take some skill and no small fortune to beat him

RAVEN   **FIGHTING SKILL**   10
                               ENDURANCE   12

If you have the Codeword **CORSAIR,** after the first round of fighting, turn to **68**
If you have the Codeword **FENCE,** after 2 rounds of fighting, turn to **61**
Note down this reference.
If you win, turn to **35**

172

"These are Seth" (the man in black half bows, mockingly), *"and Enoch. I know you recognize Enoch"*

The man in blue looks down at you, pure hatred in his eyes.

"He certainly remembers you, as you used him as a puppet to kill his protégé. He really wants your blood, but as long as you do as he says, then you will be safe."

Enoch's scowl deepens, his eyes never leaving you. He may yet betray his mistress.

*"**Enoch and Seth** will take you to where you hid this item. They are my most trusted lieutenants, and will have no compunction to slit your throat if you lie. Especially Enoch. Understand?"*

All reasonableness has fled out of Lilith's voice, which now sounds cold and emotionless.

Turn to **137**

173

You thought you thought of something of interest, but then it's gone out of your mind. You must be too tired, you think. You need a good days sleep. You return to your pallet and turn fitfully until sleep finally takes you.

YOUR ADVENTURE ENDS HERE (FOR NOW)

But if you want a sneak preview of Shadow's next caper, turn to **176**

174

You turn and see the woman from the One Eyed Rat standing on the rooftop, not 10 yards from you. She is now wearing all white, except for black boots and a black shirt. At her side are two short black swords. Lilith smiles,

"So here were are again. You have cost me dear, tonight, Shadow. You have cost me some valuable men, ones that it will take time to replace. However, I am not bitter. If you have the item, then give it to me now."

You stand up and face her.

"Why should I?"

"Well, you are a thief, are you not? You care for money, is that not so? The Kindness are rich, we are paid well to take people into the deathly embrace of our mother. If you give the item, then I will give you all the money you will ever need in exchange."

You are very tempted, but still are not sure. Can you trust an assassin? However your options are limited.

Will you:
Fight Lilith, turn to **145**
Accept Lilith's offer, turn to **65**
Throw the item to the cobbled streets below, turn to **90**
Throw the item into the waters of the harbour, turn to **103**

175

The wind takes you and you do not have a chance to react. You fall, your hand reaching out desperately for the thin cable. But it's a futile attempt.

The drop is three floors, but you have got far enough across to be over the garden. Before you reach the ground, you hit the trees.

You scream in pain as your shoulder is pierced by a short branch, but your momentum keeps you falling. You tumble down the trees trunk, being scratched and impaled in several places.

Then you drop to the ground with a thud, blood bleeding from multiple wounds. Your head hits hard and you are in a daze. You shake your head and try to get up, but realise you cannot feel your legs.

Looking down, you see that you are impaled just above the waist by an old fence post. The sharp point has severed your spinal cord, and no power on earth can help you move your legs.

A shadow falls over you, and you look up, still too stunned to be in pain.

A giant half-orc grins down at you. He grabs you, and wrenches you off the fence post. The pain starts, and its excruciating. You howl in agony. He dumps you to the floor, and grabs hold of one of your useless legs, by the ankle.

He drags you around to the front of the house, towards the guard's quarters. He grunts to himself, thinking how well he and the lads will eat tonight.

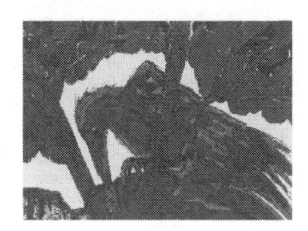

TONIGHT WAS YOUR LAST ADVENTURE

176

ACT ONE: MURDER MOST HORRID

The high, starched collar itches terribly. You resist the temptation to reach up and scratch your neck as you stand there in the large reception room, holding a silver tray, filled with silver goblets of the finest red wine.

The silk job that Lecas tipped you on worked well a few nights ago, and netted you a good profit, plus Lecas got his 15% cut. Then Jacs found you in the One Eyed Rat, toasting a successful venture with Lecas.

He had heard from a girl he knew that there was a large party in the upper city. The richest and most important men and women in the city would be present, as well as the high ranking members of the church and local government. Everyone would be expected to be there for the beautification of Arch Cardinal Devero, who so brutally murdered in his own quarters. You remember it all too well, as you were a suspect for some time. You also know that the beautification will have little effect, as poor Devero ended up damned to hell.

It had been hard going, but you and Jacs had managed to get the necessary paperwork: identification papers, contracts of employment and travel passes. It hadn't been cheap, and it was one of the biggest operations the Jackdaws had launched this year, but the rewards were too big to ignore.

You managed to be hired as a member of the waiting staff, named Anton. Your long, dirty hair had been washed, trimmed, combed and waxed. It's pulled back into a neat bun at the base of your neck. You stubble had been trimmed into a neat, short beard. You even wore a pair of wire rimmed spectacles to complete the image. They had plain glass in them, as your eyesight did not need any help. However, they did have a special tint to them.

You are in a fine (for you) black three piece suit. Both the waistcote and the jacket were buttoned up, and underneath was a heavily starched white shirt, and a black silk tie. You feel like you are being throttled. On your feet are a pair of polished patent leather shoes, which pinch you toes.

You look around once more. The reception room is a good two hundred yards long and one hundred wide. Its walls are papered in rich, textured patterns, and portraits of the great and good hang on the walls in thick gold frames. The roof is ornately painted, with scenes from the holy book, despite this being technically a government building. The lighting is a series of wall lamps, the latest in modern engineering, as they are all supplied by pipes with petroleum gas, and could be turned off and on at the same time.

The room is on the ground floor of the Parliament building in upper Amaldi, next to the basilica. The Parliament may be traditionally secular, but nothing in the city escaped the interest of the church.

The building is a squat tower shape, which goes up for six floors. On top of this in the roof, live the famous Rooks of Laeveni. For centuries, since the tower was build, they have nested there. They are now so ingrained in the public consciousness, that if one shits on you, it's considered good luck. There is also a legend that if they ever leave the tower, the whole city will fall. It is forbidden to hunt them, kill them or even wave them away. If they wish to feed at your windowsill, or from your table, you cannot shoo them off. For this reason, the Parliament building is more commonly known as the Rookery.

You hear a cough and force yourself back to the present. You look around and see the maître-de, a small pompous man named Phillipe, trying to get your attention. As you look over and he frowns, and points with his fingers that you had been hired to move around the room, offering wine to the guests, not just loiter and daydream.

The room is full of at least 200 people. There are priests, politicians, merchants and the landed gentry. You move through the room easily, stopping to present your tray. The guests help themselves to wine that's 10 gold pieces per goblet, but all ignore you as you bow your head in respect and deference to them.

The women were necklaces and bracelets of gold and platinum, diamonds and rubies. The men have gold cigarillo cases, silver fob watches and ceremonial knifes at their waists. You catalogue everything as you move through the room, for later. You reach the centre, and glance up and see Jacs heading your way. Sorry, Auric.

He is carrying a similar platter, but his is filled with fresh fruits that he has to slice for the gentry.

You don't make eye contact and ignore each other, and soon he passes you by. You move around, going back to the bar counter to get fresh glasses of wine.

You see a number of high ranking churchmen and women working the room, trying to drum up support. There were at least seven of them vying for Deveros now vacant post. The Arch Deaconship was an important role in the church, and did not come up often. You find their campaigning distasteful. Strange, you think, how a thief can have the moral high ground over ranking Church officials. But in reality, death, respect and mourning waited for no one in the cut throat world of Church politics. You only met Devero once, and briefly, but you remember him fondly, as he had gone to extreme means to protect the city, even by selling his souls to save Laeveni.

On the left you see Arch Bishop Craven trying to impress some of the large landowners, no doubt promising a cut in land taxes if he is elected. Further on, Monseigneur Favera tries to woo a group of merchants, no doubt promising to slash import tax. You cannot see Malombr amongst them and absently wonder if he survived his ordeal.

However the largest group hovers attentively around Father Brandon. Surrounding him are merchants, landowners, soldiers and fellow clergy. He talks easily, with good humour and a quick wit. He gets easy laughs from his audience, and holds them rapt as he tells them stories from the psalms, but without sounding sanctimonious or patronizing. He is indeed a man of the people.

That's apparent because his plain white cassock marks him out against the others. For he is a simple parish priest of the poor quarters, but much loved in the lower city. It is rare, but not unknown, for a man of such modest rank to rise to such a prestigious rank. The smart money amongst the bookmakers is that he is the favorite.

He is neither a letch, not larcenous. His interest in children is purely for their physical, mental and spiritual well-being. He is not a drunk, a philanderer, or a snob. He is universally liked, by poor and rich, merchant and solider, pious and sinful. From little you know, he would make a fine Arch Deacon.

You check on your tray, and see that you are down to about two glasses. You walk past Father Brandon's group to refill at the cark counter, and pass within a few feet of him. Then all of a sudden the lights go out, all at once, plunging the room into darkness. There is a buzz of confusion, and you are jostled by the crowd as they start to panic. Then there is one scream. Moments later, the lights flicker back to life.

On the floor, face down in front of you, lies Father Brandon. A red stain is spreading across his pure white cassock, in a rough circle from an area between his shoulder blades. His head is facing you, and from the floor you see his grey eyes stare out, seeing nothing except maybe the next world.

You sigh. What a waste of a good man. Then you feel something dripping down your arm and you look to your tray. There are two full glasses, and another that has fallen over the in confusion and spilt red wine on the tray. That must be it.

You look across the room and see that Jacs is standing only a few feet away, on the other side of the dead body. He is staring down in shock at the body, and hasn't noticed that something is also leaking from his tray. At first from this distance, it looks like its juice from the beets he has been slicing. But then your sharp eyes notice on the tray a wooden handled knife in the centre of the pool. It's the paring knife he has been using to slice the fruit. Its short, with only a 4 inch blade, but that blade is clearly covered in a liquid much thicker and more viscus than vegetable juice. Its blood – and it's dripping onto the floor.
It's only a matter of time before someone notices, and blames Jacs for the murder.
What will you do?
 Will you..................BE A PART OF SHADOWS NEXT CAPER?, IF SO THEN WATCH OUT FOR:

"*A Parliament of Rooks*"
Coming soon from Black Dog Gamebooks

177

You swing through the air towards the house, but soon you realise you are dropping too fast. You have miscalculated the angle of the swing, and you are heading to a ground floor window.

You brace yourself for impact, trying to put your arms in front of your face as you hit. You crash through the leaded glass window. You feel several pricks of pain where the sharp edges cut you.

You continue falling forward and let go of the rope. All hope of stealth is now pointless. You roll and jump to your feet, reaching for your sword. Blood drips freely from several long gashes in your arms and legs.

You look around, and sigh in despair, as you realise you have managed to break into the guard room at the bottom corner of the house. Several half-orcs have stopped playing cards, arm wrestling, and swigging foul ale.

They all turn towards you and grin, their fangs making the expression grotesque. They advance towards you. There are too many, and they can smell blood. Man-flesh is on tonight's menu.

TONIGHT WAS YOUR LAST ADVENTURE

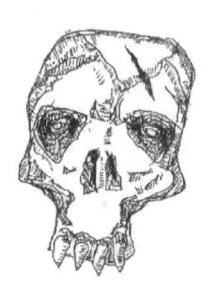

177

You leave the hideaway, and make your way through the sewers to the nearest ladder up. Unseen a dark shadow jumps out behind you, two steel swords swinging. Fortunately, as fast as he is, you are faster. You dodge out of the way, and then climb swiftly up the ladder. The Raven follows, but as it reaches the surface and pokes its hooded head through the manhole, you stab it in the eye with your belt knife. The body falls down the hole and lands with a splash.

Gain 1 **FORTUNE** point

Turn to **66**

178

You wonder what to do with the rest of the evening, now your plans have been disrupted. Then you feel a sting in your neck. Damned mozzies. Always bad by the harbour. But then you fall forward, to the hard cobbled floor.

You head a female voice talking over you,

"He clearly did not have it. Return to the merchant's house and tear it apart. I want it back. Tonight. No matter the cost."

"*Yes, dread lady"*, replies a deep voice.

TONIGHT WAS YOUR LAST ADVENTURE

179

You lean against the wall of the alley, panting with the effort. Then you leave. You head straight to the safe-house where you stored the mysterious object in earlier in the night. You run across the rooftops and drop into the attic of the local bakery run by Leff Rawls. You recover the item from a hidey hole. You think about opening it. You decide otherwise. You put it inside your jacket.

"Hello Shadow. It is very kind of you to lead me to it direct. I don't know how to repay you."

You turn to see Lilith standing by the hatch to the attic. Flanking her are Seth and Enoch.

"Ah, I know! You are a thief, are you not? You care for money, is that not so? The Kindness are rich, we are paid well to take people into the deathly embrace of our mother. If you give me the item, then I will give you all the money you will ever need in exchange."

She gestures to Enoch, who pulls out a heavy purse from inside his tunic. He opens it and shows diamonds glittering inside. You nod in agreement.

"You first, dear boy", she insists.

You take the item from inside your tunic and pass it to her. She smiles, and caresses it lovingly. Then she gestures to Enoch. He throws something at you. It glitters as it flies through the air. And then another item. You catch them both with quick reflexes and open your hand.

In it are two small silver pennies, worth next to nothing.

You look up in shock, and start "*But*-"

Enoch's blade interrupts you as he runs you through. Lilith smiles,

"Two silver pennies to put on your dead eyes, to pay the undertaker, and the ferryman in the next world. As promised, Shadow, all the money you will ever need"

TONIGHT WAS YOUR LAST ADVENTURE

180

You reach out and pull the right lever. A large bag of flour drops from the ceiling, where it had been hanging by a rope. It flattens Seth, who falls with a cry. The 100 pound bag snaps his neck, and he falls to the floor, dead. The bag and Seth's body are between you and Enoch. You dart forward and grab hold of Seth's sword, and pull it from his scabbard.

"Now we will have a reckoning, runt", he smiles, without humour.

ENOCH   **FIGHTING SKILL**   **12**
                             ENDURANCE   **10**

If you have either of the Codewords **CARDSHARP** or **DESPOILER**, then Enoch gains 1 **FIGHTING SKILL** due to his thirst for revenge. If you have both, he gains 2 **FIGHTING SKILL**

If you win, turn to **169**
If you lose, turn to **166**

181

The god of luck must be turned away from you, as when you withdraw from your most recent attack, your front leg slips off the ridge. You seems to hang there for an age, but then gravity takes over. You try to grab onto a hanging sign as you fall.

TEST YOUR FITNESS
If you pass, turn to **165**
If you fail, turn to **149**

182

The flaying claws and sharp teeth of the Dusk Devil are too much for you. It is also preternaturally fast, and you struggle to fend it off, but too little avail. You start to slow, as the venom on the animal's claws starts to have an effect. Its normal pray are smaller mammals, and so it takes time for it to get into your blood stream and nervous system.

But your vision starts to swim, and you stagger. Your knees buckle and you drop to the floor, defenseless. The Dusk Devil hisses in delight, and creeps over to you on all fours. It prods you with its claws, and you can do little but weakly wave an arm towards it. Like a cat playing with a mouse, it continues to move around your body, prodding you, until you are too weak to respond.

Then you hear a mewling noise from the other side of the room. The Devil disappears from sight, and returns shortly with a small creature clinging onto its back.

It's a baby Dusk Devil! It looks down at you curiously, with large eyes. Then its mother picks it up by the scruff off the neck, and places the baby on top of your chest.

Paralysed and helpless to move, all you can do is watch, and groan in pain, as the mother teaches her baby how to slowly carve sweet bits of flesh from your body.

The baby quivers in excitement when it is fed its first food apart from mother's milk – human flesh. After a few slivers of dripping red meat, it starts to pick at the large gashes that have opened in your torso. Then it crawls up your body, still mewling, eyes wide, until it reaches your face.

The baby cocks its head to one side, curiously, and then it reaches out a small paw, claw extended. It starts to prod at your left eye, until it finally pierces the eyeball, and you can feel the aqueous humor run down your face. The baby leans in and starts to feast.

You have become a feast for a new born babe, and it will be a long and painful feast for you.

TONIGHT WAS YOUR LAST ADVENTURE

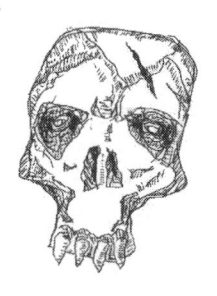

183

You move a fraction to slow, but that's enough to seal your fate. The blade slices easily through your thin neck. Blood spouts from the wound, and your head arcs into the dirty water of the sewer with a splash. Your body topples into the filthy liquid.

The Raven leaps down lightly into the water, making barely a ripple. She grabs hold of your body by the belt, and pulls it to the edge of the sewer. She roughly searches your body, and finds nothing.

She will not be happy. Orders were to capture the little thief, but he was out of reach and the killing stroke was the only option.

The Raven turned, preparing herself as this may be her night to go to the Dark Mistress, along with the thief. But she will not be welcomed into the realm of death as she has failed. Such are the prices for consorting with the dark powers.

TONIGHT WAS YOUR LAST ADVENTURE

184

Three trained killers was too much for you to cope with. After putting up a valiant effort, you are eventually cut down, a vicious slice across your neck.

You drop to the floor of the dark alley, as blood pools around you. You feel hands searching you, but sense frustration as they do not find what they seek.

You die not knowing what the strange item you stole was, and why it has cost you your life.

TONIGHT WAS YOUR LAST ADVENTURE

185

The brawl is getting increasingly violent. Your opponent knocks to you to the floor, and you land heavily. You are knocked clean out for a few seconds, but then you start to drift back to consciousness. Your eyes flutter open, and all you see is a giant form heading towards you.

Someone has brained a half giant with an oak table (no mean feat) and the huge creature staggers towards you, its eyes unfocused, and its legs like rubber. Then it trips and falls, straight onto you. The huge being crashes on top of you, fracturing several of your ribs. You struggle to breath, and feel your mouth fill with blood as your lung is punctured.

The half giant is knocked out cold, and you try to push it off your body, but your arms are pinioned under the huge body. Your breathing becomes increasingly ragged and shallow, until it finally stops.

TONIGHT WAS YOUR LAST ADVENTURE

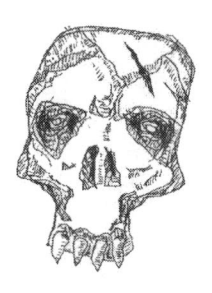

186

You decide to head to the front door and leave. This place is not worth the trouble you have invested in it. A key skill in being a thief is knowing when to walk away, and all your instincts tell you that the time to leave is now.

You dash down the stairs as you head another dreadful scream from above, and go to open the door. However, your fear has paralyzed your mind, and you do not stop to check for traps.

You unbolt the door and unlock it, and eagerly turn the handle to freedom. As you do, a thin fibre breaks attached to the handle, a fibre that was at maximum stretch. When it does, a small bag of fine paper falls to the floor.

In it is a mixture of small stones, cannon powder and other substances. As it hits the hard floor, the stones scratch against the powder, and there's a "*bang*". The parcel flares open, and spread by the small explosion is a fine dust, which drifts up towards you in a cloud. You cannot help but inhale it.

The poison works mercifully quickly.

TONIGHT WAS YOUR LAST ADVENTURE

187

The first thing you notice is that you can hear voices, three of them. There's a women's voice, and two men, but they are talking so softly you cannot make anything out. You keep your eyes closed, so they don't know you are awake, and concentrate on your other senses.

You are obviously upright and seated. Your head is slumped down onto your chest, your long hair covering your face. You can feel the burn of rope in your wrists, where threads of the rope dig into your skin. You imagine your feet are also tied.

The room smells of incense and blood. This does not bode well. Then you try to listen again, but cannot make out the conversation.

Then you hear light steps moving over the floor towards you.

"Come now, Shadow, I know you are awake. You cannot play possum with me. Now raise up your pretty head, and let us see you."

The voice is a woman's, rich and deep, and one you recognize. You see no point in pretending. If they had wanted you dead, you would be already, and so you still have a chance. You raise your head, your eyes blinking in the light.

Standing over you is Lilith. She looks down at you, smiling.

"Good boy. You have led us a merry dance tonight, young Shadow. You have some talent to avoid us for so long, but yet, here we are", she smiles again.

"You must be wondering why you are still alive. Well, it's very simple. You have something of ours. We know you took it from the Merchants house, as I can feel that it was in your possession. But you have obviously hidden it. Where is it?"

"What is it?" you ask, hoarsely.

"Never you mind, Shadow, but it is of great worth to The Kindness, and to me personally. If you can return this to us, then we will reward you well. Will you help?"

She sounds very reasonable, but there's something hidden beneath her courtesy, and it makes you nervous.

If you decide to help, turn to **6**
If you don't trust Lilith, and hold out, turn to **85**

188

Just as Shadow opens the escape hatch and slid down it, at the other side of the attic, there's a crate stuffed with straw. A small form is snuggled in the hay, and wakes up at the noise. She peers over the side of the crate, wiping sleep from her eyes.

She sees mummy looking scared, and then sliding down a hole, soon followed by another thing, which looks mad. She sees another creature draw a metal thing and wait to go down the hole. She senses that this creature means mummy harm.

Soot climbs from her crate, where she has been sleeping since mummy brought her here for safekeeping. She launches herself at the nasty creature, and her small but sharp talons scratch him twice on the neck, near the carotid artery.

He screams in pain, and tries to swat Soot, but she is too fast. She scurries away and the nasty creature jumps down the hole. Feeling sleepy again, and thinking she has done all she can, Soot climbs back into her crate and is soon asleep.

Turn to **190**

189

"Now we will have a reckoning, runt", Enoch smiles, without humour. Moments later, Seth also drops into the alley. You must fight them both.

ENOCH	FIGHTING SKILL	12
	ENDURANCE	12
SETH	FIGHTING SKILL	11
	ENDURANCE	14

If you have either of the Codewords **CARDSHARP** or **DESPOILER**, then Enoch gains 1 **FIGHTING SKILL** due to his thirst for revenge. If you have both, he gain 2 **FIGHTING SKILL**

If you win, turn to **134**
If you lose, turn to **11**

190

"Now we will have a reckoning, runt", Enoch smiles, without humor. However, moments later, Seth also drops into the alley, but he lands on his arse. He stands up, unsteady. Two small cuts are visible on his neck, and blood seeps from them.

"Whats the matter, man?", demands Enoch

"Nothin", says Seth sullenly, his voice slightly slurred. However, they both advance on you. You must fight them both.

ENOCH	FIGHTING SKILL	12
	ENDURANCE	12

SETH	FIGHTING SKILL	11
	ENDURANCE	10

If you have either of the Codewords **CARDSHARP** or **DESPOILER**, then Enoch gains 1 **FIGHTING SKILL** due to his thirst for revenge. If you have both, he gain 2 **FIGHTING SKILL**

But…
When Soot scratched Seth on the neck, then she introduced a toxin into his bloodstream. It's not enough to kill him, as Soot is only a baby. However, it's slowly affecting him, and so every fighting round, Seth will lose 1 **FIGHTING SKILL**. This may be the difference between life and death for you.

If you win, turn to **134**
If you lose, turn to **11**

191

You go to switch the glasses, and you think she didn't notice. However, before you can react, she picks up the glass on the left, leaving you know choice but to pick up the one on your left. She raises it towards you, and says "*Salute*". As its tradition, you clink your glasses together. Then she downs her whisky, and watches you.

Under pressure you drink your glass dry in one go. She smiles slightly when you place the empty glass down.

"Anyway, I must be away. It was a pleasure talking to you.", she says, and stands and leaves. It was a strange encounter that leaves you somewhat perplexed. You cannot decide if you are sad that she's left, or relieved.

Turn to **91**

192

If you have the Codeword **FALCON**, turn to **109**
If you do not, turn to **64**

193

You are sick of sneaking around, and decide to try to fight your way out. There's only two of them and they look normal. You resolved to charge at them,

If you have the Codeword **HEISTER**, turn to **133**
Otherwise turn to **144**

194

You use your **SKILL OF CHAKRA**, but it's hard on your body, as it uses the energy of your body. You concentrate, placing the palms of your hands on your chest. You feel heat from your hands as you channel your body's strength. You start to burn the toxin out of your body.

It hurts like hell.

TEST YOUR FITNESS
If you pass, then you succeed in cleaning your body of the toxin. However lose 1 **FITNESS** from the effort. Delete the Codeword **CROOK**. Now turn back to your previous reference.

If you fail, the toxin takes hold, and you die.

195

You leap to the side, just in time. There is a click and something fizzes past your head, and buries itself in the wall behind you. A trap! You might have known. You were lucky, but it makes you want to see the contents of the drawer even more.

You pull the draw fully open. Inside you find a ledger. You skim through it and see a list of dates, numbers and coded entries. The numbers you assume are price's in gold pieces. The coded entries may relate to clients, goods and addresses. If you decide to keep the journal to examine later, add it to your Adventure Sheet. You also find a purse. You pick it up and shake it.

Roll 1d6 and times that by 10 – that is the amount of gold pieces you find in it when you open it. You put this in your bag. At least you have something to show for tonight's work.

Also there is a vial of clear glass. You hold it up to the limited light and it appears to be a blue green liquid. There is a maker's mark on the bottle and a rune. You open it and the odour makes you queasy and drowsy. You quickly replace the stopper, but it's too late. Your eyes get heavy, and you start to feel sleepy. You nod off briefly, and sleep for about 10 minutes, but then you awaken. You were fortunate you didn't inhale more!

You have found a **POTION OF SLEEP**, which can either be inhaled or drunk. Add it to your Adventure Sheet.

There's nothing further of interest and so you quietly close the door and reset the trap by removing your pick. You head for the door.

Turn to **40**

196

Its bedlam in the room, as everyone fights anyone, be they friend, family or unknown. Chairs fly across the room, or are smashed over heads. Beer tankards and wine goblets are hurled. Soon you are faced with an opponent.

Using the table below which one it is from the number you threw earlier.

Roll	Opponent	Fighting Skill	Endurance
1	Dwarf	8	10

You find yourself in front of a squat but broad dwarf. He has a long, brown beard, indicating he is likely to be relatively young (under 100) and so maybe a bit more impetuous that older dwarves. He is wearing chain mail, over a leather tunic, and slung on his back is a large doubled edge battle axe.

His eyes light up when he sees you,
"Aye, laddie, you do not look like you will last long. A bit of a taster before I find someone truly of worth to tussle with", he grins, ***"Rest assured lad, Dewey will rock you to sleep."***

With the he raises a large, gnarled fist, that seems almost the size of your head, and throws a fierce haymaker punch at your head. Can you knock this sturdy dwarf, Dewey, out?
This will be a fight of **ENDURANCE**, and so if you have a **FITNESS** of 10 or over, you can add 1 to your **FIGHTING SKILL.**

2	Barbarian	8	12

You look up and see a huge shadow fall over you. In front of you is a huge barbarian, at least 6 foot 6 tall, clad in furs and scraps of chain mail. She looks down at you and laughs,

*"**You a scrawny excuse for a man. Sheldra will knock you out with one blow. HA HA HA**", she laughs.*

You don't doubt her. She is all muscle and long arms and legs. Your only hope is probably speed and agility. If you have the **SKILL OF SPEED AND AGILITY**, you can add 1 to your **FIGHTING SKILL**.

| 3 | Man in Blue | 9 | 13 |

You find yourself faced with the man you saw start the fight, and you realise that it was a distraction to get to you. In every way he's an average looking man. Height, weight, looks. However there's a coldness to his eyes, and he moves with a relaxed litheness. He is dressed in a smart doubled breasted blue tunic, well made, but not so fine that it stands out. He is dressed that he can pretty much fit into any part of Laeveni's society, unremarkable, and instantly forgettable. He wears tall leather boots, and at his waist is a long rapier.

He says nothing, but smiles thinly at you, and then drops down into a wrestling stance, arms outstretched, and then he lunges at you. He is fast, like a striking snake. You will have to be patient. If you have the **SKILL OF FORBEARANCE**, you can add 1 to your **FIGHTING SKILL**

If you win this tussle, write down the Codeword **DESPOILER**.

| 4 | Ogre | 7 | 14 |

You find yourself face to face with an ogre. These creatures are ape like, in their arms are as long as their legs, and they tend to walk on all fours. It's dressed in nothing but a dirty loin cloth, and its body is powerful with a thick torso, a large belly and sagging pectorals. Its legs and arms are long, but thin, but still contain terrible strength.

Ogres are not great conversationalists, but its pig like eyes light up when he (or her) sees you. She (or him) swings a large fist at your head.

Ogres heads are notoriously as thick as the stone they lover to burrow into, and so using your brain is your best bet in this fight. If you have an **INTELLIGENCE** of 9 or over, you can increase your **FIGHTING SKILL** by 1.

| 5 | Man in Brown | 7 | 11 |

The man in brown you noticed entering earlier pushes an almost unconscious Halfling out of the way and stands before you. He says nothing, but straight away drops into a fighting stance. He looks well practiced.

You will need a bit of luck to beat this man. If your **FORTUNE** is 9 or over, you can add 1 to your **FIGHTING SKILL**

| 6 | Goblin | 6 | 8 |

The goblin before you is one of the few creatures in the room that you are taller than. It's barely half a foot over 5 feet, and its skinny and scrawny, with a long hooked nose, pointed ears, and large yellow eyes. Its green grey scaly skin is clad in basic leather armour.

However, Goblins are notoriously dishonorable and this one has drawn a short knife, which just fits between his dirty fingers. Any hits from this foe will inflict real damage to your **ENDURANCE**. You do not need to roll 1d6 for the goblin is it hits you, as any strike will inflict 2 **ENDURANCE** points which you will not gain back later.

As you cannot use a weapon, then your **FIGHTING SKILL** is reduced by **TWO** for this fight. However, if you have the **SKILL OF UNARMED COMBAT**, then it remains at your normal level.

Note down your **ENDURANCE**, as it will not be permanently affected by this fight. The fighting occurs as normal, but this time, you have to role again for damage.

Whomever wins each round, rolls 1D6, and consults the below table.

Roll	Blow	Effect
1	Straight punch	1 ENDURANCE
2	Straight kick	2 ENDURANCE
3	Uppercut	3 ENDURANCE
4	Roundhouse punch	4 ENDURANCE
5	Roundhouse kick	5 ENDURANCE
6	Knock Out punch	Knocks out opponent

If you win, turn to **112**
If you lose, you are knocked unconscious, if you have the Codeword **BRIGAND**, turn to **138**
Otherwise, write down the Codeword **LARCENER**, and turn to **129**

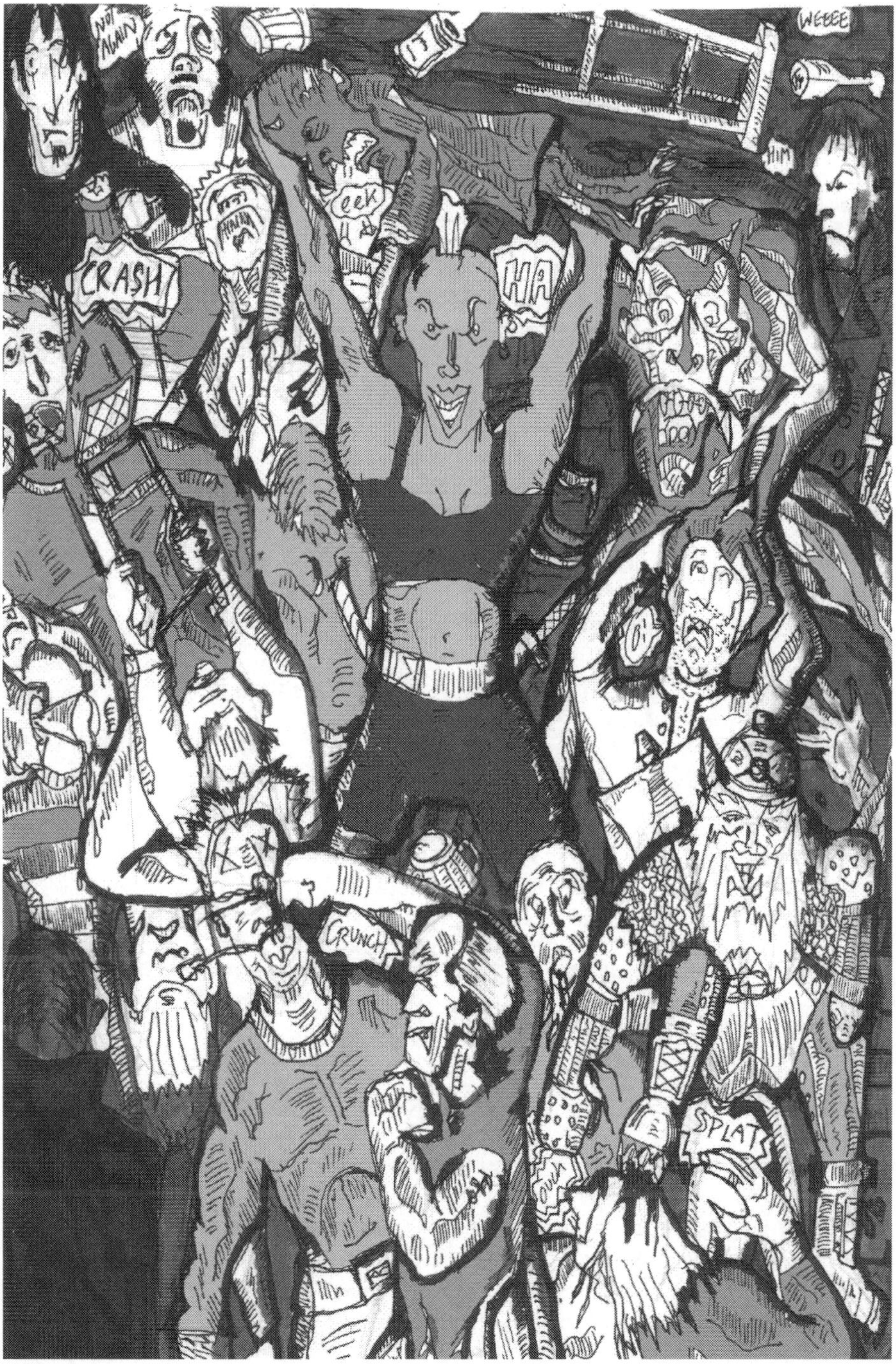
NOT AGAIN
WEEEE
eek
CRASH
HA
CRUNCH
SPLAT

197

You do nothing and climb up into the attic of the bakery.

He hasn't found the hatch yet, and so you open it, and go to slip into the room.

Enoch puts his arm across you,
"**Me first, rat**." he growls, and he slips through the hatch. You decide to follow. Seth is not far behind.

You are in a dark and dingy loft. There is no window, and the ceiling is low and beamed. There's a brick wall, that's part of the chimney from the bakery below. Despite the early hour, master baker Leff Rawls, is hard at work, as the bricks are warm as the ovens below bake the day's bread.

"Where is it?" demands Enoch

"Over here", you point and start to lead. You walk to the wall, and pull out a brick, showing two levers.

"I just need to pull these, and the compartment will open." You explain, pointing at the levers *"Or would you rather do it?"*

He looks at you, trying to decide if it's a trap.
"**You do it**", he orders.

You have two choices:
Pull the left lever, then the right, turn to **141**
Pull the right lever, then the left, turn to **180**

198

You notice the back cover of the journal is noticeably thicker than the front. You inspect the leather, and notice that close to the spine, that the leather stitching has been unpicked. It's so close to the spine, it's almost impossible to see. You run your fingers down it, and your fingertips fit in the gap. They feel a thin sheath of paper.

Carefully, you pull the paper out. Its fine parchment. Folded. You carefully unfold it and examine it. It's a list. There are four headings: name, item, cost, information. But everything else after that is written in code – one that you cannot immediately make out.

Are you going to try to break the code? You reason it may not be useful tonight – but maybe it would in the future.

Name	Item	Cost	Information
Ixgbkt	Uvoas	1,000 GP	Jxam Gjjoiz. Hxgtjut Qtkc
Lgbkxg	----	----	Kshkffrkx. Hxgtjut Yayvkizkj
Lmtggbl	Uhgwtzx Xjnbifxgm	250 GP	Knfhnk hy Wxobe phklabi
Spek	----	----	Glmph Efywiv. Zmgxmq gsrjiwwlhxs Hxgtjut
Xkyzgr	Orrgigur cnoyqe	500 GP	Griunuroi. Hxgtjut Qtkc
Qsxx	----	----	Kec. Mr pszi amxl qepi wivzerx. Gsrjiwwih xs Fverhsr.
Chotgdt	----	----	Vhgftg. Axkt mh khu khhdxkr

YOUR ADVENTURE ENDS HERE (FOR NOW)

But if you want a sneak preview of Shadow next caper, turn to **176**

199

Quickly, you take the stairs down to the ground floor, and head towards the front door. There is also a single door on the right of the hallway.

If you have the Codeword **MOONLIGHTER**, or you just want to leave the house now, you ignore it, and unbolt the front door and slip out into the street. Above you a shadow watches.

Turn to **79**

If you do not have the Codeword **MOONLIGHTER**, you can decide to try the room. You start to open the door.

Turn to **99**

200

If you have a journal on your Adventure Sheet, turn to **131**

Otherwise, you and Lecas discuss the silk shipment over another beer. **YOUR ADVENTURE IS OVER, FOR TONIGHT**.

But if you want a sneak preview of Shadow next caper, turn to **176**

Running a tavern in Laeveni, even a well ordered, well run tavern such as the One Eyed Rat, it's not easy.

Join landlord Lecas as he tries to keep order, and keep happy the variety of barbarians, dwarves and wizards that frequent his tavern. Grab yourself a pint of Necromancers Black Heart, and visit the best tavern in the docks.

TAILS FROM THE ONE-EYED RAT
BY LOWRIE
MM
ME
ME
ME
ME
MEEP
ME
ME
ME
ME
RIGHT, WHO'S NEXT
ME
MEEE
ME
ME
ZZZZZZZZZ
©LOWRIE 2014
A QUIET NIGHT AT THE ONE-EYED RAT

WHAT HAVE I DONE?
LECAS' FIRST ATTEMPT AT SHOWING LIVE SPORT WAS NOT A SUCCESS
TAILS FROM
TONIGHT ONLY
THUNDER LIZARD BOXING
LATE
RULES - NO BITING, NO KICKS NO TAILS. PUNCHES ONLY
YAWN
ROUND 47
©LOLMIE 2021

OH FOR ZACATECAS' SAKE NOT AGAIN!
© LOWRIE, 2021
EEK
TAILS FROM THE ONE-EYED RAT
BY LOWRIE
GRYGH S STCK N DR GN
GARYAGAH. I'VE TOLD YOU YOU HAVE TO USE THE BACK DOOR
SRRY LCS
CAN SOMBONE BRING ME THE GOOSE FAT
HOW MUCH?
ALL OF IT!
IT'S OK BIG FELLA
C'MON
HEH HEH
WITH SUCH A BIG HEAD
YOU'D THINK HE'D HAVE A BIGGER BRAIN

WORDS & PICTURES BY LOWRIE
TAILS FROM THE ONE-EYED RAT
TIME TO SPEND A GROAT
CREAM
TROLLS
HUMANS
GOBLINS
GIANTS - PLEASE USE THE STABLES TO STOP THE DRAIN BLOCKING
AGAIN
DWARVES
HOBBITS
NOT AGAIN
WHY IS IT ALWAYS A DWARF? SOME SORT OF INFERIORITY COMPLEX?
©LOWRIE, 2021

TAILS FROM THE
ONE-EYED RAT
BY LOWRIE
WHAT DOES GANDOLFI LOOK LIKE?
IT'S SO 2941
SO CLICHED
SO STEREOTYPICAL
GIVES WIZARDS A BAD NAME
HEY, I'M A MAGE
AND, I'M A WARLOCK
YEAH, OK
SIGH, MAGIC USER?
©Lowrie2021

WHAT HAVE I DONE? AGAIN?
TAILS FROM THE ONE-EYED RAT
©LOWRIE 2021
TONIGHT ONLY
THUNDER LIZARD
ARM WRESTLING
8-LATE
BOO
BORING

TAILS FROM THE ONE-EYED RAT
BY LOWRIE
ONE WHISKY, ONE BRANDY AND ONE GIN AND TONIC
DEADIST
I'M SORRY... I DON'T SERVE SPIRITS
©LOWRIE, 2021

TAILS FROM THE
ONE-EYED RAT
BY LOWNIE
IN THE KITCHEN
HELP
TABLE 15 ARE ASKING WHERE THEIR KRAKEN IS
PFFT.. I AM AN ARTIST! MY CREATIONS TAKE TIME
BUT WHEN?
THURSDAY?
SNIFF
MAJOR
©LOWNIE 2021

ONE NIGHT, A GROUP OF ADVENTURERS DECIDED TO COMPARE THE ODDEST THINGS THEY'D HAD TO FIND TO COMPLETE A QUEST
TAILS FROM THE ONE-EYED RAT
BY LOWRIE
WHY?
HIC
OGRE DUNG
KOBOLD SICK
GAMLI'S ROCK NOW
THIS STINKS
STUPID FOWL
MAMA AND PAPA
© LOWRIE, 2021

WORDS & PICTURES BY LOWRIE
TAILS FROM THE ONE-EYED RAT
© LOWRIE 2021
MORNING, ZIL. WHAT WILL YOU BE HAVIN'?
HULLO, LECAS. WHAT HAVE YOU GOT?
WEDNESDAY NIGHT BLOOD-DOLL
THURSDAY SINGING NIGHT
FRIDAY 6-6 UNHAPPY HOUR
NH 7%
OD ?
LPA 5%
WIPE
LPA, A HOPPY PALE ALE, NECROMANCER HEART, A GOOD DARK PORTER, AND ORCS BLOOD A...
I'LL TRY THE ORCS BLOOD
YOU SURE?, IT'S MA...
YES, ORCS BLOOD LECAS
SLURP
HMM
BLEE
THAT'S FOUL! WHAT'S IN IT?
ORCS BLOOD

NOT AGAIN
THEY HAVEN'T EVEN STARTED PLAYING YES
OF ALL THE FIXTURES IN THE ANNUAL INTER-SPECIES CRIBBAGE LEAGUE, THE MATCH BETWEEN THE ORCS AND DWARVES WERE ALMOST THE MOST "COMPETITIVE"
CRACK
TAILS FROM THE ONE-EYED RAT
BY LOWRIE, ©LOWRIE, 2021
DWARVES RULE

ZOMBIES WERE ONE OF LECA'S FAVOURITE CUSTOMERS
TAILS FROM THE ONE-EYED RAT BY LOWRIE
BRAINS
BRAINS
BRAINS
THE USUAL THEN?
THEY ALWAYS WANTED THE SAME DRINK
AND THEY NEVER TALKED ABOUT POLITICS OR RELIGION. OR ANYTHING EXCEPT BRAINS

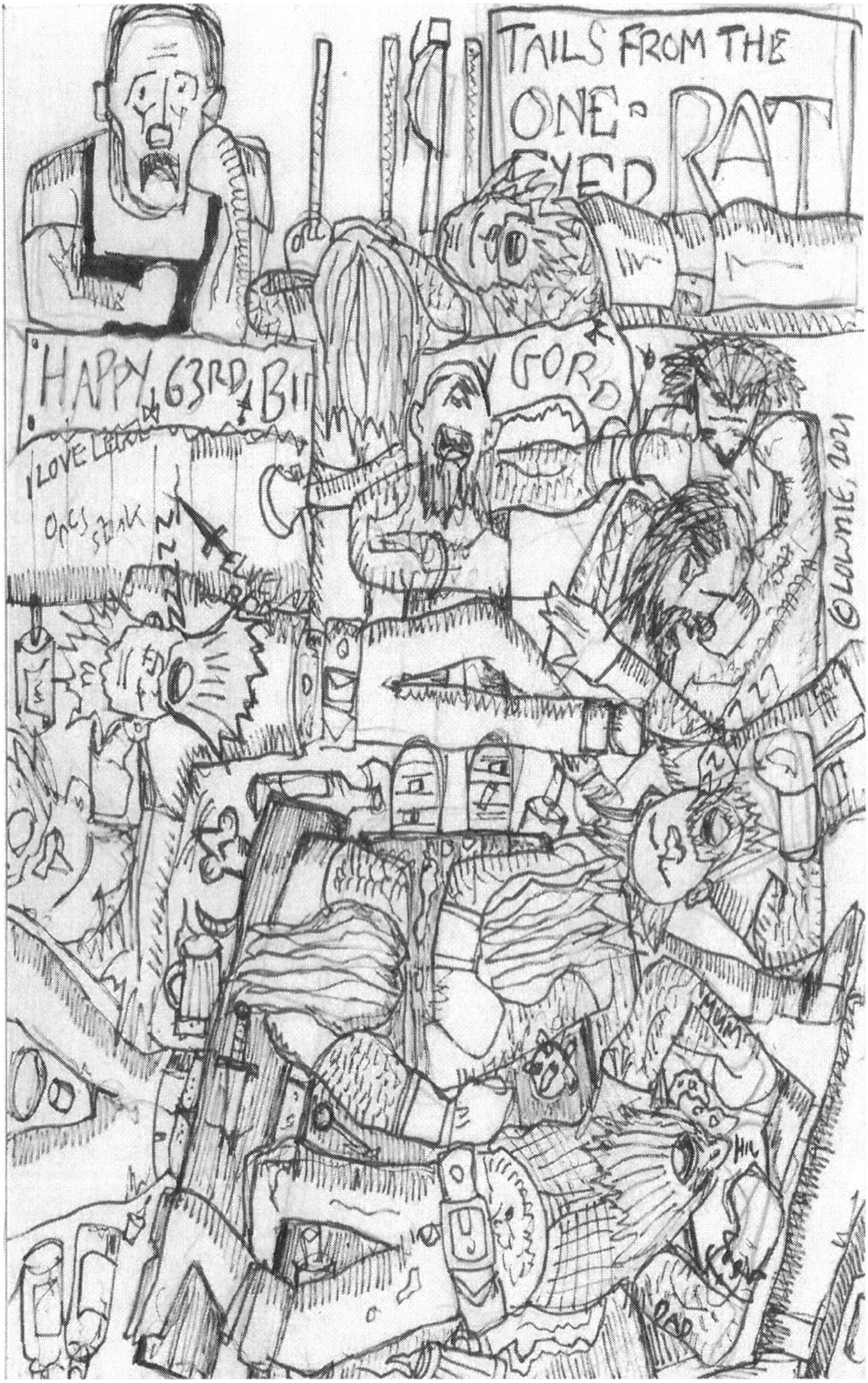
TAILS FROM THE
ONE-EYED RAT
HAPPY 63RD BI
GORD
©LOWMIE 2021

THE TAIL OF HOPPIT THE ONE-EYED RAT
PART 1
TAILS FROM THE ONE-EYED RAT
BY LOWRIE
ANOTHER HOPPIT?
EEEK EEEK
HOPPIT USED TO BE A FAMOUS BARD CALLED HARPETTO
HE WAS TALL, BLONDE AND HANDSOME WITH A VOICE LIKE HONEY, MAIDENS LOVE HIM.
HE GOT INVOLVED WITH THE YOUNG WIFE OF A MERCHANT... OR SO HE THOUGHT
WHERE IS HE?
EVERYONE ELSE HATED HIM, FOR THE SAME REASONS
LITTLE DID HE KNOW THE MERCHANT WAS REALLY CHIEF OF...
THE UNKINDNESS
LOSER
ARSE
POSER
PURSUED BY ASSASSINS, HE FOUND A HALF-DEAF WIZARD, AND PAID HIM TO MAGIC HIM TO HIS FRIEND LELAS
TAKE ME TO THE ONE-EYED RAT
REALLY? YOU..
YESS, NOW
OK, THE CUSTOMER IS ALWAYS RIGHT
BAMPH
TBC

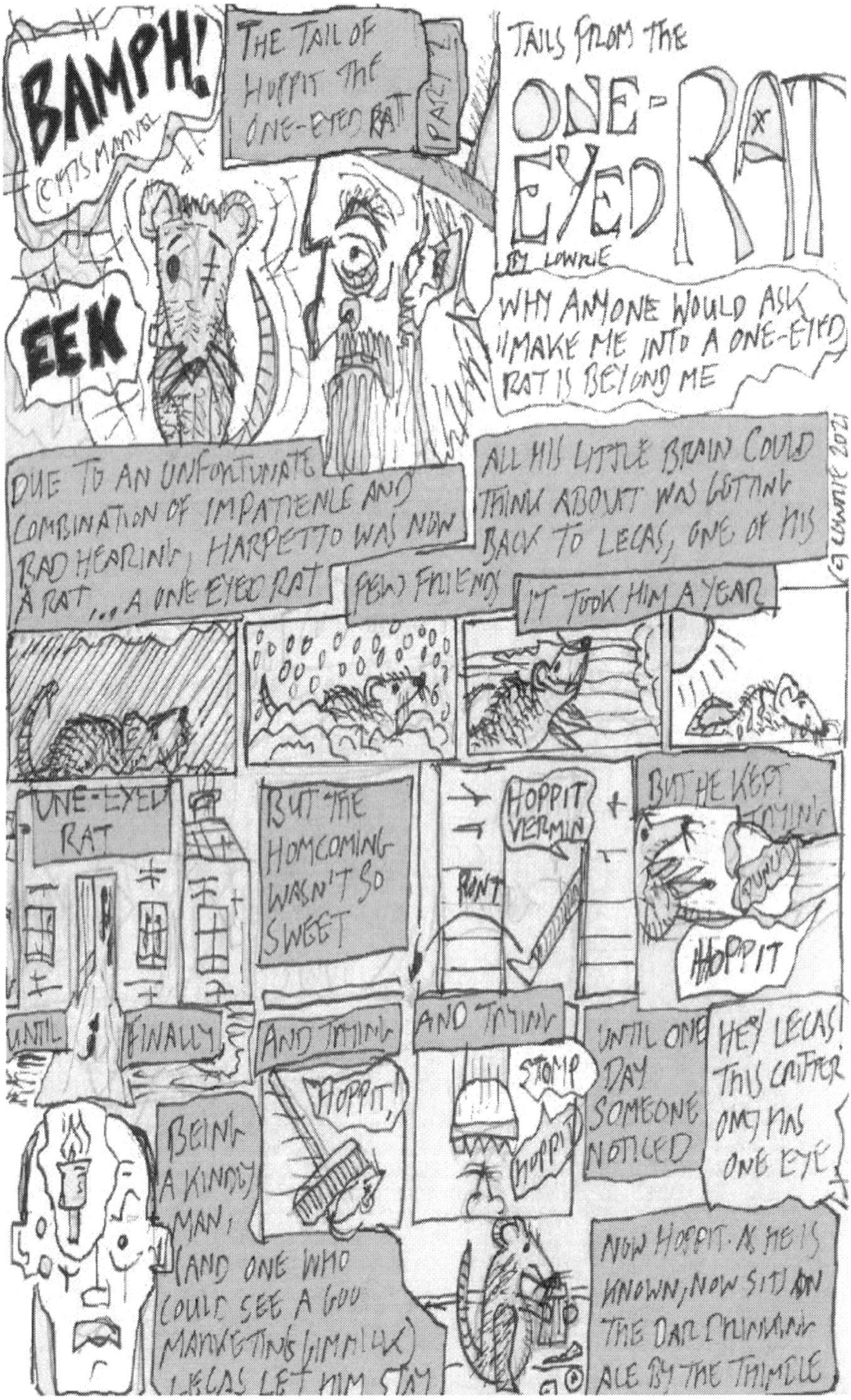

LOWRIE'S
TAILS FROM THE ONE-EYED RAT
SORRY LITTLE MASTERS YOU'VE BEEN
TAVERN WATCHED
ARAGON
ELRIC
BANNED
PIPPIN
SAM
FOR TORN PILLOWS, LOSS OF PONIES NOT PAYING THE BILL
THEFT
SHADOW
THAT WAS AGES AGO
WHAT? STILL?
WELL, AN AGE AGO
THAT INCIDENT IN BREE? WE WERE BARELY INVOLVED
PO-TA-TO
BLOODY BARLIMAN

LOWRIE'S
TAILS FROM THE ONE-EYED RAT
TONIGHT ON DWAR TOSSING
OK, I ADMIT IT'S A BIT CULTURALLY INSENSITIVE CAN I GET YOU BOYS A DRI
DOWN WITH THIS SORT OF THING
BOYCOT TH ONE-E
NO-ONE TOSSES DWARVE
RAT

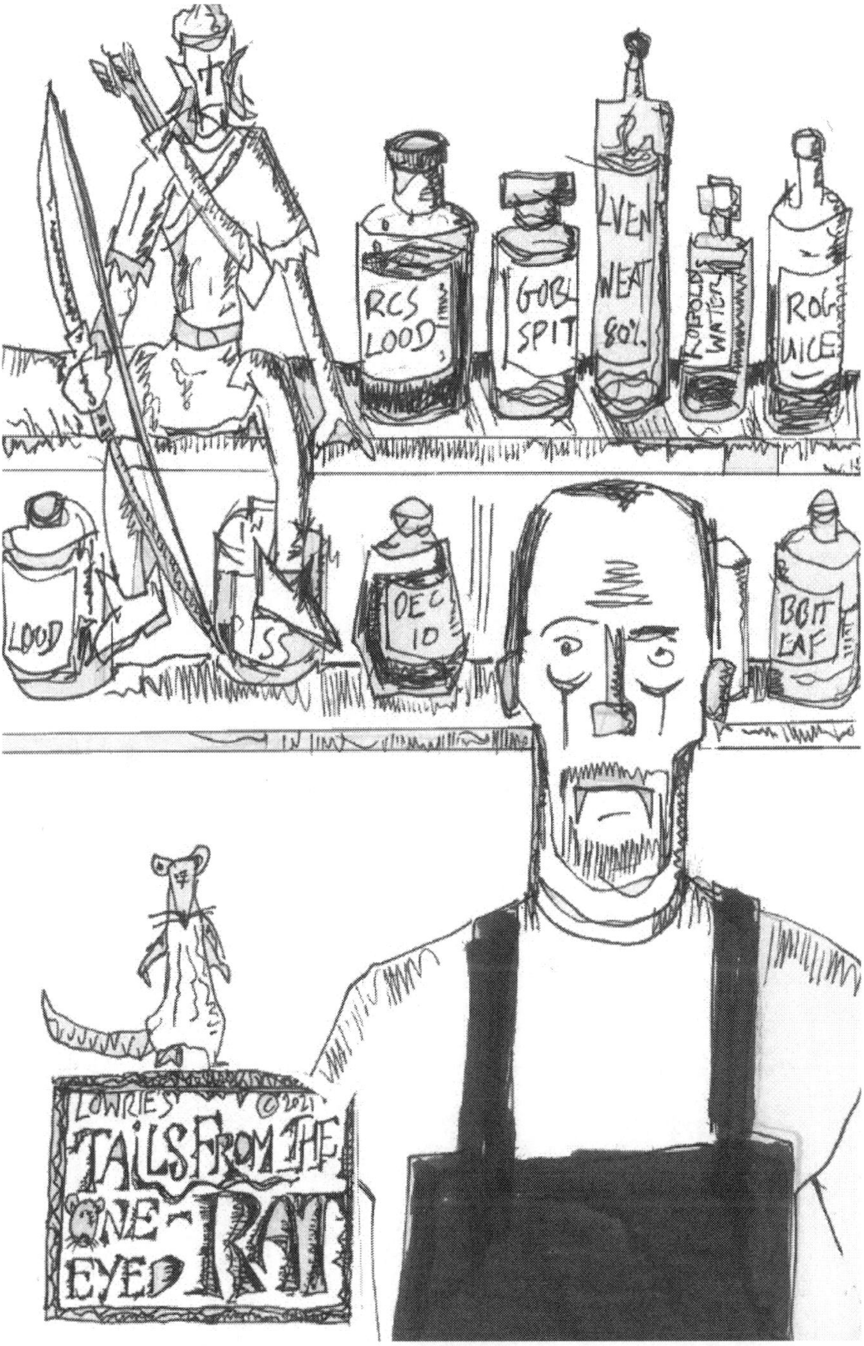
RCS LOOD
GOBL SPIT
LVEN WEAT 80%
ROG UICE
LOOD
OEC 10
LOWRIE'S ©2021
TAILS FROM THE ONE-EYED RAT

LOWRIES
TAILS FROM THE ONE-EYED RAT
NECROMANCERS HEART
DARK WICKED
-STOUT-
7%
GET OUTTA MY PUB!

THE GREAT ONE-EYED VARNEY / RAT CROSSOVER
VARNEY THE VAMPYRE
THE ONE-EYED RAT
©LOWNIE 2021
ELF WEE
ORC SNOT
THIS SATURDAY THUN ARM
DAMN VAMPYRS, THEY NEVER PAY...
LOOK INTO MY EYES. YOUR WILL IS MY WILL. YOU WILL GIVE ME A GLASS OF AB- FOR FREE
& RHYMES WITH BAD CIDER
AH, A 1664, LOVELY
IS THAT IT?

THE MONTHLY ALL SPECIES C.A.M.R.A MEETING WAS ALWAYS A HEADACHE
LOWRIE'S TAILS FROM THE ONE-EYED RAT
CAN'T BLOODY WIN
eek
NOT ENOUGH SULFUR
WHAT!
NO SLUGS OR SNAILS?
ELF WEE
TROLL SPIT
NEEDS MORE BLOOD
WEAK AS KOBOLD P**S
NOT BITTER ENOUGH. NEEDS MORE LEAF

Cough Cough
LOWRIE'S TAILS FROM THE ONE-EYED RAT ©2021
WELL MET, STRIDER
WELL MET, LOW LEON
RANGER TEAM MEETING
3 HRS BEFORE DAWN
BREAKFAST NOT INCLUDED
WELL MET, LEAN SHANKS
WELL MET, ERM...?
KEVIN
I'M NEW
WHEN DO I GET A COOL NICKNAME? AND A PIPE?

LOWRIE'S ©2021
TAILS FROM THE ONE-EYED RAT
DAMNED DAEMON-BREED
THEY ALWAYS WIN
GW
TONIGHT-CHILLI EATING CONT
1,000,000 MILLION SCHOVILLE UNITS
IS THAT IT?

LOWRIE'S ©2022
TAILS FROM THE ONE-EYED RAT
HELP!
PROPERTY OF SHARKS
QUICKLY LANDLORD, 4 SCORE PLATES OF MEAT STEW. TO GO. (BLOODY RANGER) WE ARE IN A HURRY
NEW
VEGETARIAN & VEGAN MENU
STARTS TODAY
Oh....
dammit
LOOKS LIKE MEAT'S BACK OFF THE MENU, BOYS
WHATS A MENU?
SORRY LADS
FISH STEW
FISH AIN'T A VEG-E-TABLE
Oh
TOFU CURRY PLEASE
DO THEY DO SMASHED AVACADOS?
HEART HEALTHY OMLETTE?
ANY PO-TA-TOES?
BLOODY ELF FOOD
HOPE THEY DO B&B&B
ANY QUINOA?
NOT EVEN WAFER THIN DWARF?
DUST?

Printed in Great Britain
by Amazon

045af7c2-8736-45a5-8242-40002742a8afR01